The Unfound

J.W. Garrett

Available from Black Hare Press

DYSTOPIA

AFTER THE FALL - BOOK 2 by STEPHEN HERCZEG
THOSE THAT REMAIN by MATTHEW CLARKE
HEIST by ALEXANDER NACHAJ
AN EARTH THAT KNOWS MAGIC by J. KRAWCZYK
THE UNFOUND by J.W. GARRETT
DRUMMING FOR THE DEAD by GABBY GILLIAM
MASSACRE ON THE MANHATTAN EXPRESS by J.D. DOOLAN
BLUEBELLS by LEANBH PEARSON

Black Hare Press
linktr.ee/blackharepress

First published in Australia in April 2022
by Black Hare Press

Edited by Jodi Christensen
Formatted by Ben Thomas
Cover design by Dawn Burdett

For after the battle comes Quiet. Humanity had been strong, energetic, and intelligent, and had used all its abundant vitality to alter the conditions under which it lived. And now came the reaction of the altered conditions.

—H.G. Wells, *The Time Machine*

Contents

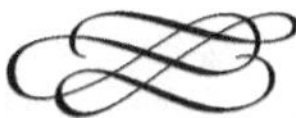

Sometimes ignorance is bliss. Until it isn't.

If anyone were to ask about the first day—the day I knew—I'd say something like it was raining or lunchtime or I had just spoken with a client. All petty details. Because what came afterward made words too difficult. Forever changed the innocent way I viewed the world and those given the responsibility and the power to lead us.

Simply put, it was the day my soul died.

—Ellie Adams

1

Scott Adams

The sun brushed the horizon, scattering pockets of yellow and orange, chasing away the remains of the night. At this time of morning, hover cars only dotted the air below here and there, nothing compared to the gridlock that would soon bring the morning's traffic to a standstill, the security bots' flashing lights bleeding red.

Raising my fourth cup of coffee to my mouth, I gazed over the city that would resemble a war zone in a matter of days—a week tops. Hard to believe, given the temporary serenity in front of me. It had taken the better part of the night to admit I wouldn't be here when that happened. But my family would, if I could get to them in time. And harder still, within the limited time frame, to ensure they understood what was at stake.

Years of accumulated knowledge at my fingertips and only now the reality slapped me in the face. I drank in the serenity of the sunrise from fifty stories above the city. From this vantage point, I could almost believe it was all a lie. Deceived, like the masses of people going about their daily lives below. Until recently, I'd been one of them.

Time was a precious commodity, for me anyway. I lingered a few minutes more as the sun burst from its nightly cage, formally awakening the day. In a way, I was a metaphor for this new dawn. Newly awakened. Here, then gone. The clock was ticking. A lot needed to transpire before nightfall. I hoped I'd last that long.

My intercranial device buzzed in my head. A message. These nagging bits of hi-tech the civilised world had clung to as lifesavers, were not that. In fact, they were the antithesis of that. But, with all pertinent information right there, ready to access via mind link, the public couldn't resist. Greedy for more, they lapped it up—me included. I couldn't help the dark chuckle that left me. The last twenty-four hours had been pure hell. Not one sliver of this damn diabolical scheme would have worked without this scrap of hardware meshed in our brains.

Society had already been hooked by the time these things became mandatory at birth, in the year 2035. By then, the little marvels of technology were deemed essential. We were almost a cashless society. However, cash was still king today in those small underground communities, where, for a variety of reasons, people had avoided the insidious things.

For the rest of us, the IC apparatus had become so engrained for daily living that to get by—to purchase, sell, communicate, transact business, monitor health—you had to be connected. I wondered if the beginnings of this horror coming for us now had been birthed way back then, with the inception of the devices.

With our cyborg assistants, synthesised beings, AI, and VR all intricately interwoven into daily living—all *necessary* components, you see—we basked in our ability to maintain our life of ease, and in the process, assisted in manufacturing our own demise. But we were too busy tracking the minutia of our lives to notice.

Now in the year 2055, looking back, who could have stopped this train wreck coming to fruition? All this time necessary for the meticulous strategies to unfold, while a patient Inner Circle added fuel to the fire, growing stronger in their power over the people, more confident in their fastidious rule, painstakingly mapping out each step toward their ultimate goal. We, the people, were too blind to see and could never have conceived of the threat anyway. And now it was too late for most of them.

I was too far among the fringes, not privy to the inner workings of the tightly knit conspiracy, although I'd been led to believe I had a seat at the table. For the past fifteen years, here in DC, I'd worked with those in the highest level of our government, beginning the day we formally became the Perfected States and moved to a more cohesive union. Or so I thought.

I activated the incoming message with a double blink and listened, not because I cared what anyone wanted of me at this point, but because I had to steer clear of any interference until I finalised the details imperative to my personal agenda. One that gave my family a fledgling chance at life.

Scott, you're needed at a meeting at 2:00 p.m. Don't leave me hanging. We're in this together. Remember that, man.

Sighing out my pent-up breath, I glanced at my solar-powered watch. Just after 6:00 a.m. I'd be long gone by two. But my friend Jeremy would be the recipient of my old-fashioned package by mail in two days' time, one which contained actual *paper* documentation. Our personal discussions, the data we'd uncovered, and this rare gift would lead him toward a well-earned opportunity, if he decided to take it. And I hope he did. If he made it through, the man had the ability to chart a way forward. He'd be my choice. But I needed to give that particular piece a rest; my focus was required elsewhere, lighting here and there on parts of the plan as yet undone.

Like Mason, former Inner Circle, and another loose end. A long shot maybe, but I'd have to trust him to implement his next step on his own. This item was crucial, if civilization, as we knew it today, would exist in any recognisable form in the future—if we were to have a fighting chance. Without him, my eyes might never have been opened to the truth; and, even now, privy to the atrocities about to be unleashed, I still can't wrap my head around it all. Taking the risk to help us humans, Mason forfeited life with his kind; my instinct told me he'd come through for the rest.

The sound of construction pulled my attention back to the span of windows lining one entire wall of my office. The grinding metal screech combined with the steady whir of the machinery's mechanics bored into my head. Dread burrowed in my gut as I witnessed the beginnings of the giant Jumbotron installations that would eventually deface the landscape of every major city. Dread, not for me, but for the millions of people who weren't prepared for what came next, this first outward step advancing sooner than I'd anticipated.

Naturally, their immediate concerns would turn toward their families and the catastrophic losses that would suddenly ensue. Wrapped up tight in their own personal cluster of tragedies, they'd never understand what they'd given over long ago had led them right here, and they were powerless to stop it.

I rubbed my eyes, clearing my vision in the face of the looming monstrosities and willed strength into my body for the hours that lay ahead. It was too soon. Would I be ready in time? An alert buzzed my IC device. As expected, the president would address the states this evening. That oughta be good. Too bad I had other plans.

The timetable, though, felt escalated. I couldn't be too late, not when I finally had worked out almost all the pieces to my own elaborate scheme. My thoughts drifted to the stark reality of what lay ahead for me. Even armed with the foreknowledge I had, that would only be a distant echo when compared to the harsh existence tomorrow would bring.

My IC device had been activated. I was already one of them—the Lost. Though I was privy to that information, the process hadn't been turned loose yet. Too dangerous to be kept around, my memories intact, me and others like me who represented too high a risk were marked to be first.

This initial display would convince the grieving public that anyone could succumb to the mysterious illness, all important to the plans of those at the top, as the devices we'd welcomed into our lives turned on us all, one by one. The real truth, what this elaborate charade masked, wouldn't unfold until later. Until the majority of the population had already succumbed, divesting themselves of this unique, one-of-a-kind resource. At that point, the divisions between the Lost and the Found would only matter to a few.

I turned back to the chaos of my desk, feeling like the ticking time bomb that I was. Clearing the clutter of my mind, I returned to the tasks that could only occupy me for the next few hours. I had to be finished by then. I felt the weight of each one of the precious minutes left, needing them to give my family the best odds possible. Maybe one day, with the perspective of time and new life, they'd see the coming days and their aftermath through a different lens. But for that to happen, mandated that they survive the onslaught first.

Nothing could prepare my family for what was about to occur, how their lives would shatter, armed with the knowledge that I'd failed them in every way imaginable. But maybe, just maybe, by slogging through this morass, I'd also hammered out a path for life. In the end, for any chance at all, for a remnant to survive, those people had to be cognisant of the truth, providing a way forward for those who remained. For all my failings, at the very least, I could give them that…

Oddly enough, as the minutes flew by, my confidence in my plan solidified. As the horrible truth had come to light during the past two weeks, the only thing keeping me putting one foot in front of the other was the hope that my wife and my son would not only survive the initial deluge, but would endure way beyond.

Without a doubt, I had the perseverance and determination to get through this day for them—Ellie and Wyatt. But, Jesus…what came next… I had to think of it like my own personal cure, or I'd not have the courage to see it through.

Ellie Adams

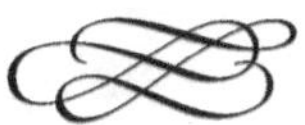

I parked and grabbed the groceries from the back seat, then scooted my way to the door with my arms full. Why was Scott home? It wasn't even 1:00 p.m. Maybe a late lunch? Maybe he'd taken the afternoon off? Looked like my surprise homemade dinner wouldn't be such a surprise anymore. I'd even gone cold turkey on our cyborg personal assistant for the night, leaving me with total control of the buying, preparing, fixing, and serving of said meal. Dangerous territory—I felt positively invigorated, like a pioneer woman. I couldn't even hazard a guess as to when I'd last personally prepared a meal.

Scott had been distant the past few weeks. Brooding, tense, uptight. Not like himself at all. But I had a plan. Wyatt would be out for the evening. So, we'd have the place to ourselves. I stumbled through the door and immediately met stoic stares from Scott and Wyatt in the den. Wyatt? Why was he here? Whatever was transpiring between them had jacked up the tension in here. I guess I'd have to shuffle to Plan B. "Wow. What world problems are you solving over there? Want to put them on hold long enough to give me a hand?"

Scott pasted on a smile and walked into the kitchen. "Ellie, you're home early."

"Stop that. I can tell something serious is wrong. What did he do that would bring you home in the middle of the day?" I asked, my brows raised, eyeing my son. Scott's eyes held a storm of emotion I couldn't translate as they met mine. "That bad, huh?" He shrugged and set down the groceries he'd taken from my hands.

Scott jerked his chin in some silent signal to Wyatt, who scooped up a leather-bound book on the coffee table and slid from the couch.

"Wait, Wyatt," I said to his retreating back. "Whatever is happening, we should talk about it together. Wyatt..."

"What happened to your day full of appointments?"

Scott prodded.

"The life of an event planner… I finished them early. I get a few easygoing clients every now and then." I could see he wasn't listening to my response, unusual for him, no matter how preoccupied he was with work.

Pushing aside the groceries, he hung his head and took my hands in his.

"Scott, what is it? You're scaring me. Is Wyatt sick or hurt?" My mouth dropped open. "Did he get someone pregnant?"

"It's not our son," he said, slowly searching my eyes. "It's me. You need to prepare yourself and be strong for him. This will be hard to hear. Hell, it's hard to say." His voice turned raspy. "I have a whole speech prepared…"

"You're sick? God, no…"

"In a manner of speaking."

"Stop talking in riddles."

"Come with me."

I fell in line behind Scott, my mind scrambling, focusing on his broad shoulders that shifted as he walked. The ones I'd leaned on daily during our nineteen years of marriage. Something was different in the way he carried himself today. Whatever it was had been eating at him for weeks, but we hadn't had time to discuss it. So, we'd fight it together. Just as we always did.

I marched into the bedroom we shared, charged by my own personal pep talk, as Scott heaved a breath and pressed his weight against the door. “Now that it’s time, I’m not sure where to begin.”

His weak attempt at a smile scared me even more. “Jump in wherever,” I encouraged, my voice light, hopeful.

He reached for my hand, and I joined him on the bed. “Nothing in our life is as it seems, and everything you thought you knew is about to change.” I opened my mouth to speak, but he shook his head, his stone-hard gaze meeting mine. “Let me get this part out first, okay?”

With a deep breath, he began again. “I’ve known for a while something big was up, but it wasn’t until two weeks ago that the truth started to unfold. The more I uncovered, the more unravelled. I had to work in secrecy to gain as much information as possible to help you and Wyatt. My time’s up. But your new life starts today…tonight.”

I blinked, willing his words to make some kind of sense. “What do you mean, your time’s up? Do those huge screens going up have something to do with this?”

“I’ll get to that, and yes.” Another deep draw of breath. “Ellie, the mechanisms inside our heads, the IC devices, will activate soon, beginning with those of us holding governmental positions, who are no longer held in good graces. Me. And thousands of others. Then the assault will continue, moving to individual family units. Those on the inside want this…condition to appear contagious, arousing fear and panic, sending people indoors, isolating them.

He squeezed my hand. “There’s no way to stop it once

it begins, and it already has for me. What happens next is vile. Memories erode, taking anywhere from a day to a week to just…evaporate. These nasty things embedded in our brains transmit the memories somewhere else. I never figured that part out. For viewing on those jumboscreens first, then collectively our memories will be stored."

My hands trembled. Scott was intelligent, his IQ off the charts. That's how he got his coveted position to start with. But my husband was clearly delusional. This couldn't be the truth. "Scott? You'll be okay. I'll get you some help." I raised my hand to cup his cheek. "You've been working too hard."

"Baby, we haven't got time for that shit. Don't condescend to me. I won't be okay, but maybe you will. Everything I've done the past few weeks was to find the best chance at life for you two."

My throat tightened as I tried to decipher what was coming from his mouth. "But there's always hope." The words stumbled from my lips, soft and meek. "Right?"

"Not this time." The muscles along his jaw strained. "Not for me and the millions who will follow. We'll be lifeless, empty shells."

"But they found a cure for Alzheimer's twenty years ago. This sounds like that. Maybe…"

"No. It's not a disease. They're mining our bodies for memories. They'll frame it as an illness to keep people compliant, stupid, and scared for as long as possible."

I threw my arms around him. Somehow it felt like he was already checking out on me, and we hadn't even begun to fight. "I'll take care of you. For better or worse, remember?" He allowed the embrace for a few seconds, his body tense and rigid against mine, then gently disentangled himself.

"I know it's hard, but you must accept it so you can move on to what comes next. There is no outcome in this scenario where I improve. The switch has been flipped for me. Think of it like that. On… Off… We need to get those things out of you and Wyatt before you share my fate. If that happens, everything I've uncovered, the risks I've taken, will have been meaningless, and I'll have failed completely."

"I'll get help. We'll go to the top. Stop at nothing."

"There's no one to go to. And the problem is at the top—in the Inner Circle. And they're the ones, the upper echelon, pulling the strings. They'll watch everyone fall, then reap what they've sown."

My mind raced. I needed to fix this. Whatever this was, we *all* had to survive it. Because life without Scott wouldn't be living at all.

"I can see your mind working. That's good. Hang on to that. You'll need it in the days ahead, for you and Wyatt."

"You talk like you won't be there. However long you've got, you should be with us, Scott."

The only acknowledgment he gave me was a thin press

of his lips before continuing. "Government resources won't help you. They'll be covered up in housing the Lost. That's what they'll call them, appropriately so. Those whose memories have been transferred...wiped clean. Going forward, technology isn't your friend either. Anything that keeps you connected with the outside world needs to be shut down, eradicated completely.

"Over time, we ceded control of bits of our lives, then eventually more and more, so much so we don't even recognise the power we've surrendered. It was a slow trickle at first. I guess that's why we allowed it. That's why we didn't notice, and we've been bleeding ever since. Question everything, Ellie. Don't have faith in anything you've been led to believe in the past."

"The Lost," I repeated, my mind gravitating toward the phrase.

"The code name for this undertaking is The Lost and Found. Those who succumb—the Lost. Those who do not and were never meant to—the Found. Then those in between, who were meant to be one of the Lost but didn't fall prey? They are the Unfound. That's where you and Wyatt come in. You, and others like you, will fall through the cracks of their wretched plan to rise again one day."

"Wait..." My mind felt like it was circling the drain. "Who are the Found?"

"That's it." A tiny smile touched his lips. "Now your brain's kicked in. The Found are the Inner Circle, those in ultimate power who've orchestrated this entire mess, slowly moving their plan toward culmination, likely over the course of many decades."

"But why? What's the endgame?"

"My guess is our memories will be used to bargain for more."

"Like what?"

"I've detailed my thoughts on this. And it's not pretty. You can read it later."

"God, Scott. I can't imagine a life without you."

"You must. For Wyatt."

No… My eyes filled at the same instant my stomach lurched, and I ran to the bathroom, sick. The cold water I splashed on my face and drank down shocked me into the brutal reality Scott had so vividly painted. When I lifted my head, he stared back at me, reflected in the mirror, and handed me a towel.

I collapsed into his arms, crying, while we swayed to a slow silent rhythm. Time passed until our chests stopped heaving and my breathing slowed. "How long do we have?"

"You can't afford to waste any time at all. I can already feel the effects hitting me, and I won't be condemned to walk around lifeless, until some random act ends my agony some other way. I need to close that loop myself, as soon as I've given you both the best odds I can."

Nodding against his chest, I tuned in to an actuality

that I couldn't even imagine just this morning. Echoes of the years we'd spent together spun through my thoughts. "I'm not as organised as you. I'm sure I'll screw this up."

He lifted my chin with his forefinger. "You and I both know that's not true. Ellie, you're truly my better half."

"I don't agree." I gave him a firm shake of my head. "But, for sure, you're the glue. I'm never gonna be okay again."

"You're a fighter," he gritted out. "And so is our son. You'll make it. Just like I feel what's coming, I know that to my core."

"Wyatt… What did you say to him?"

"Not much. I didn't want him to bolt. He knows we're in danger and that I can't be with you. That book I gave him has all my notes and documentation. Plus, a plan for your escape and where you should go first for surgery. Most people won't know the IC devices we've been depending on for decades are the cause of the mystery illness. But you two will. And don't even think of spreading the word, Ellie. You'll draw attention to yourself fast, earning a much quicker death."

"Assuming we live through that. What's next?"

"Getting to a safe place. Eventually, there will be checkpoints. People without IC devices will be picked up and "helped" along, with the final solution in mind. Staying outta sight is imperative. My blueprint for you takes that into consideration and lists a few people who might help, should you run into a bind."

My heart sped up, pounding, galloping in my chest. "Sounds like that is a forgone conclusion."

"I've literally beat my head against the wall, trying to think of all possible outcomes and the best way through them."

"I'm sure you have." I ran my fingers through his hair, pulling him closer, as he pressed a kiss to my forehead. The scent of him wrapped around me, and I drank it in. The minutes we had now would need to last me a lifetime.

"I want to be Lost, with you," I choked out.

"No. Ellie. Don't ever say that. You're the best of us. The world needs you. Say it with me… Survive…"

"I can't."

"You can. Say it."

"Survive…" I whimpered.

"That'll do, for the time being. If I know you, and I do, I'll wager you'll be screaming that soon and have our son spouting it as well."

My lips curved ever-so-slightly, my eyes filling with tears. "You are an incredible man."

"*Shh*, come here and let me love you, while I'm still me."

My heart ached with the knowledge of what the next few hours might hold. Scott was my rock. He never gave into pressure, had a work ethic that put everyone else to shame, and integrity that got him through any situation, while others floundered around him. People looked up to Scott. Counted on him. Me and Wyatt included. Steady and strong, I couldn't imagine a future without him in it.

Right now, what mattered was the time we had, the minutes and seconds between us. The breath we shared, the soft gasp of tears, his gentle touch that mounted to our desperate cries. As I trembled in his arms, the realisation hit me. I'd never be whole again less my husband.

"I love you," he whispered. "Always remember that. It's why you need to do what comes next. And I have to also."

"I love you too, Scott. I'll never stop."

J.W. BARRETT

Scott

I pressed a kiss to her forehead, then tugged on pants. Already I could feel a nagging in my head, a growing emptiness, things undone or forgotten just beyond my mental reach. *Shit*. It's advancing. I couldn't become a walking empty meat suit—I wouldn't. We needed to move this train along.

I gazed into Ellie's eyes, gone stormy, riled up with emotion. Was it sadness, fear, shock maybe? Did she comprehend it all? She had to; their lives depended on it. Shock… I couldn't let that happen. It'd paralyse her. Then she'd give into the instincts the members of the Inner Circle were counting on. To cower and hide.

"Ellie, you need to stay with me here. You can't check out. And we need to get moving, remain on task. Ellie." I shook her softly and wiped the tears drifting down her cheeks. "It's awful. Believe me. I get it. But you've got to go. Give me this peace, before I…"

Her watery gaze darted to mine. "Don't say it. Please don't say the words. I'll get up."

She threw herself at me, wrapping her arms and legs around my torso, clinging to me like she'd never let go, and God, at that moment, I wished she never would. I wish all of this could be different. I wished we could pretend away the madness coming for us all. But wishes were for fairy tales and not worth shit on a day like this. The cold, hard truth was here, merciless in its drive to defile the people. "That's my girl."

"Just a few minutes longer. Okay?"

"Okay." I dug my fingertips along the length of her spine, so I could hear her sigh against my neck, then squeezed her tight.

"I'm not sure how to even think about a future without you. So, I won't. I'll follow what you've outlined for me and Wyatt to do and take the rest as it comes."

"That's great, baby. That's all I ask. I'm so proud of you."

"Don't be. I'm gonna suck royally at this."

There she was. Revving up for a challenge. I could see the change in her eyes—a spark. What I was hoping for. That spark lets me know she'll fight, because, when that happens, she's a force to behold.

I waited for Ellie to make the first move. To disengage. When she leaned down to grab her clothes pooled on the floor and quickly dressed, I said my own silent goodbye to my partner and lover for the past twenty years. *We'll see each other again, baby. Believe it. I couldn't take these next steps if I didn't know it to be true*. I threw on a shirt and turned to face her. "Ready?"

Her troubled gaze penetrated mine. "As much as I'll ever be."

"I didn't tell Wyatt all of this. I mentioned the surgery I've scheduled for you both and that you'd need to leave. And that I wouldn't be with you. He's angry, understandably so. Help him absorb it over the next few days." Ellie nodded. "Remember. He's got my book, and I had him grab the bags I've prepacked for you both. Look through them and see if you want to add anything else. You won't be coming back here. Keep that in mind. Understand?"

She jogged her head. "You've thought of everything."

"I'm sure I haven't. Whatever I've missed hopefully isn't crucial."

Ellie grabbed the pictures on her nightstand. Two of us, two of Wyatt.

Then I took her hand and led her from our bedroom to the den where our son waited, with four travel bags on the floor, filled and open for our perusal.

Wyatt pinned me with a glare that I fully understood, even expected, and silently applauded. He would need all that and much more. I was counting on the fact that, when all this sunk in, he'd be hell to deal with. That had been his pattern since he was a young boy. For what they'd soon be up against, he needed every bit of that attitude to protect himself and his mother.

"Look over what I've packed, add anything else necessary. But keep it light. After the first leg of your journey, you'll proceed mostly on foot. I wanted you to be able to handle your bags independently."

"I've already done that," Wyatt muttered. "Quite a bit of firepower you've got us lugging around."

"Unfortunately, there's a good chance you'll need it, son."

"What's left for you? I mean, since we're leaving you behind."

Ellie tensed beside me.

"I've still got my revolver."

"The .357?"

"Yes. Drop it, Wyatt. You've got more pressing matters to concern yourself with."

"Apparently so."

"Take a look, Ellie. See that you have what you need.

I'll fix us something to eat. Then you must be on your way." I stooped to check Wyatt's bag, curious about what he'd added, if anything. What does a seventeen-year-old take with him when all he's ever known is shot to hell? I dug my way to the bottom. A few actual books—great choices…pictures, including one of our first father-son outing in the woods…articles detailing my various positions over the years…carvings that he made as a kid…the baseball from his first home run. He'd batted clean-up that day. Damn, I'm so proud of this kid. I glanced into Ellie's intense gaze. "A fine boy you've raised, Ellie."

"*We've* raised Scott. Maybe you can't see it, but he's a clone of you."

"Some days I can. Others, I see you…your spunk, your tenacity, and that makes me very, very happy." *Dinner… I was going to make dinner…*

A loud buzz filled the air, cracking, biting into the early evening. "What is it, Scott?"

"It's begun."

Ellie joined me at the window.

From our view on the outskirts of the city, we could see the giant screen light up, then heard a scratchy audio feed initiate. A random name flashed across the Jumbotron, followed by what appeared to be a memory of a wedding. "They'll say this is in honour of the victims."

"But it's devastating. To have your memories paraded for public consumption," Ellie said, transfixed.

“My theories are that this display serves a different purpose. Time will tell if I’m right or not.”

Wyatt slid in between us, his gaze locked on the playback.

“Try not to get sucked into it. My guess is this thing will run 24/7 from here on out, for two main reasons. To play on the public’s emotions and to fulfil the ultimate purpose of that monstrosity and others like it going up across the PS.”

Wyatt nodded, his expression full of unmasked dread. “I’ve started reading. Can’t say that I can fathom it all yet though.”

I pulled him against my chest and hugged him hard while silent sobs shook his body. “Take your time with it, son.” The three of us, now enveloped in a tight ball, watched the sun set in a brilliant display of orange and purple hues. Through the buzz of voices echoing in the dwindling light, I kissed Wyatt’s head and laced my fingers with Ellie’s. “What a gift you both are,” I murmured. “Despite all this, I’m a lucky, lucky man. I can’t have imagined a more wonderful life.”

Wyatt Adams

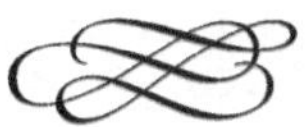

Dinner was quiet inside the house. Outside, the pouring out of memories droned on. The panic had begun, just as Dad predicted. Citizens lined the streets, waiting for the president's explanation of the unusual spectacle. Mom and Dad spoke in hushed voices, occasionally drawing me into their conversations. Dad had given us a deadline, only thirty minutes away now.

I gathered the dishes and abandoned them in the sink. Who cared about dirty plates? Not me or Mom. Certainly not Dad. I left them alone to their whispers and returned to my room so Mom could cry without an audience. Dad must have a mountain of faith to truly believe we could make it through whatever the hell was going on out there. I was pretty sure I didn't share his convictions.

Unfolding the map, I tried to focus on the first leg of our journey, the one we had to get through tonight. But all that kept running through my mind was Dad and what would take place here once we'd gone.

My dad had planned our disappearance down to the last detail, even packing two bags for each of us. One with personal necessities, the other with clothing, with room for a few items of our own choosing.

Earlier, after dismissing me to talk to Mom, I had been stunned, turning a slow circle in my room. When faced with a battle for our lives, what in this room actually mattered? How had I gone from decisions, like, who to ask out on Saturday night, to what I'd need in a fight for our existence? The stuff in here paled compared to the life-and-death concerns before us. Whatever few things I chose had to be items that would help see me through what was to come or would bring about effects that had a profound meaning in my future life.

Profound in thirty minutes or less…

Heavy shit when I wasn't even sure yet of the end game…where all this was heading. I dropped to the bed, pondering my death at seventeen. Honestly, I'd never given it much thought. Why would I? Young people didn't just die, except by freak accidents. Grandparents died. Mine already had. Less frequently, parents.

What was coming, from Dad's brief sketch of the event, amounted to a catastrophe on a massive scale. Like those occurring from natural disasters. But this wasn't that. What was headed our way had been carefully put in place, plotted out to exact specification, spanning years if not decades. And it waited for us now, like a minefield.

My hand tightened on Dad's journal. He'd said not to let it go, that I had the responsibility of making sure it left with us tonight. That, after the two of us, this book was the most important resource, to guard it with my life—we'd need it for survival.

Mom's cries seeped into the room. "Workout playlist," I announced. "Volume five." Thinking back, I can't remember the last time I heard her cry. An injury that had landed me in the hospital when I had been about ten, maybe?

Removing my sweaty fingers from the leather book, I unclasped the latch and looked inside. The pages had dates at the top, easily seen as I scanned through. The majority of the documentation had been added recently. Meeting minutes, snippets of conversations, schematics for the latest model of an IC device, lists of names and responsibilities, safe houses, Inner Circle meeting notes.

The organisation looked to be haphazard at first, until

it became clear that everything had been arranged in chronological order. The last half of the book included Dad's most recent discoveries from the past two weeks—printed out and painstakingly pieced together from multiple sources, it appeared.

Society had moved away from paper over the years. Made sense, as we were all connected through the marvel of science by the devices in our heads. A book like this would seem odd and stick out to those who saw it. But this simple book would be our lifeline now. No backup or duplicate copy. I committed to keeping it out of sight.

I lost myself in Dad's theories, detailed in their complexity and scope. A creeping horror coiled up my spine and simmered there. If all this played out as Dad had documented, it'd be a miracle if humans survived at all. I slowly closed the journal, unable to conceive the last pages my dad had written. I'd scanned some of it too fast, glossing over important points in my rush.

Why had I skipped to the end? I shivered, calculating our chances of surviving the days ahead, given the dire prediction I'd just read. Seemed hopeless to try. But failure and my parents didn't belong in the same sentence. I'd seen the determination in my dad's eyes. He believed in the data he'd gathered and had lost his chance at life with us in order to get it. How could I not fight too?

"Music off." Silence… My gaze travelled the room, and with a newfound appreciation, I rummaged through the years of minutia, grabbing a chosen few.

Dad stuck his head into the doorway, pulling me from my reverie. A chill raced down my back. Our eyes met from across the room. "I guess this means it's time."

His jaw tightened with his nod.

Outside on the Jumbotron, the tone altered, a man this time, ushering another victim's memories centre stage.

"That's right. Your mom is changing clothes." He crooked his thumb at the huge screen that I couldn't help but watch. "The commotion out there will help. Everyone's focus is on that hideous display. Security forces won't be expecting an uprising tonight, like they might in the days to come. This first evening may be the easiest in that one regard."

I wondered how he could appear so calm with what awaited him. Hesitating, I opened my mouth, then snapped it closed again. The morbid question, what I wanted to ask, hung on the tip of my tongue. I felt selfish for even thinking about asking it with the heavy weight my dad carried now.

He crossed the room as I straightened to meet him. "What is it, son? Spit it out."

"Okay." I averted my eyes, gathering courage, then lifted my gaze to his. "When it comes, if it comes, what does it feel like? How will I recognise it? I want to know, so I can prepare for my end."

"Well," he began, scrubbing a hand down his face, "in

the beginning, it's a subtle change, hard to decipher at first. Disorienting mostly. Nagging. Disturbing. But over the course of several hours, the ability to concentrate, the disconnectedness, becomes apparent. Then those symptoms steadily…worsen," he finished.

"Okay. That helps. Dad?"

His brows shot up. "Yeah?"

"I want you to know. I don't blame you. For any of it. From the little I've read of your notes, it's a herculean feat…what you've done here." I examined the floor. "And I'll never forget your sacrifice for us."

Dad yanked me into his arms and squeezed tight. "Being your dad is my highest calling and greatest privilege. The only thing that matters now is your survival and your mother's. We, humanity, need to come out on the other side of this. Godspeed, son."

All too soon, the steady buzz of the hover car ate through the silence hanging in the air. For whatever reason, the giant screens had gone quiet. Fitting… I bent over the paper map, feigning concentration on the details that lay before me. How would we ever be all right again when we had left him behind?

The devastating scene of our departure remained transfixed in my mind, and I watched it pass through my vision over and over again, as if a bystander. Maybe if I continued to see it repeatedly, one of those times the ending might change. Mom clinging to Dad. Her muted screams against his chest. Dad walking her to the car and assisting her inside. He'd kissed her once more, then strode to my side. His fierce hug calmed me. Although I can't imagine why. "You'll be okay," he announced with an air of confidence. "You both will. Be strong." I nodded while he planted a kiss on my forehead.

Words tangled in my throat. I only managed four. "I love you, Dad."

I had folded myself into the seat, still able to see him waving from the rearview mirror, like he'd done so many times before, when we were just heading out for a quick trip. Maybe that's the feeling he'd wanted to evoke, but I would prefer to think it took every last bit of will inside him not to yank us from the car and drag us back to where we'd still be under his care.

Except for the knowledge that going forward, unlike before, that wouldn't be enough. And the best way to care for us meant setting us free to face the danger alone that he knew waited for us. It felt dream-like, my last glimpse of him, standing sentinel over where our souls had resided, and then like balloons in the sky, he'd turned us loose with a little of him tucked in too.

Mom hadn't spoken a word since we'd left, her eyes focused and clear now, her teeth chewing her bottom lip, as we flew through the sky. Another voice intruded into the night. This one sounded like a teenager. I strained to hear. Shouldn't I witness what she had to say? Shouldn't someone? Her words crept out small, shaken…scared.

During all my years on this Earth, I'd never witnessed the look that crossed Mom's face. Her expression had darkened to an empty, eerie, unsettling calm. I shivered, wondering if she would be okay, able to function. And this was only the beginning of this nightmare. We sped along, with no competition for the night air around us.

The safe house Dad had secured for this first evening was close to the underground location, where we would go tomorrow. From here on out, we'd travel by foot or catch a ride. I turned up the volume of my device, casting it to the vehicle's speakers, forcing us both to listen to what our president had to say, preferring that now to the young girl's testimony, which I didn't want to internalise.

"I guess we should hear what we're up against." Mom finally spoke.

Dad had warned of the propaganda the man would spew, reminding us that knowledge of the truth would be our best defence. A rumble of voices competed for the mic initially, then only one rang through.

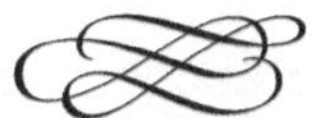

I shuddered out a breath, willing my brain to catch up with this hideous nightmare happening around me. When we'd parked, the speech wasn't done, so we sat huddled close to the speakers, listening, as each word cut further into the depths of the reality we thought we knew. I'd held out hope that Scott had been losing it due to stress, too much work, additional responsibilities. That tomorrow, after a night of uninterrupted sleep, he'd be back to himself, reasonable and apologetic about his ranting of the previous day. After dinner, he'd made me promise not to return, his gaze hard and uncompromising. So, I'd given him my word. But everything inside me screamed I should go to him. Now.

I grabbed the controls, my thoughts a jumbled mess. I needed to go home. Together, we'd sift through this shit, work through all of it. Like we always did. My hands slid, slick with sweat.

"Mom," Wyatt began, a shell-shocked tone to his voice. "What are you doing? The speech is over. Let's get out and go inside."

I blinked and glanced at my reflection in the mirror. The crazed look in my eyes felt surreal…yet well-earned. An honest response to the long hours of fear and hysteria I'd already endured. I averted my gaze and loosened my grip.

"You were thinking about going back home, weren't you?"

I nodded, not trusting myself to meet my son's eyes. "I won't though," I added, straightening in the seat, wanting to appear confident for my son. "Your dad told me exactly what that man's lies would sound like. Scott was spot-on. As much as I don't want to believe any of it, I can't fight the truth of the matter in front of me."

"Agreed."

I squeezed my son's hand, arranging my expression to what I hoped would be one of acceptance, then turned toward Wyatt. God, he was trying so hard. But terror engulfed him, etching deep lines into his face. It reminded me of his first trip up the high dive when he was six. Not the same situation by a long shot, but the feelings then were strong and real as well. I'm such a horrible mother.

"I'll be okay eventually, and so will you. One day at a time. That's how we'll confront this. I don't know any other way. Ingesting everything all at once is too overwhelming."

"Thank God, Mom. I thought you might have permanently left the building."

"Not yet. Still can't guarantee that I won't, though. Let's give today's earth-shattering events time to settle. It's a chaotic mess out there. One that we've all had a hand in creating. In some ways, that makes us all complicit. Don't you think?"

Truthfully, I was in mourning, not only for my husband but for my way of life and for the future we would never have. Tonight brought the advent of a new age that I didn't want to acknowledge, much less name or experience.

I slipped from the car, pulled my bags across my shoulders, and headed toward the door, willing my body upright for a little while longer before I could collapse and give in to oblivion. The security scan hummed to life, and I held my breath, waiting for the all clear. When both of us passed, and the door clicked open, I shuffled inside, letting the tension ease from me, along with the baggage.

Of course it would be fine. Scott had reserved this

place days ago. The worst was still in front of us. So much worse… I felt like a whisper of myself, a shadow, that, at any moment, might just be swept away.

"I'm going to take a shower. Here. Dad gave me these before I left. Now I know why."

Shoving a small box in my hand, Wyatt kept walking, exploring the place.

Earplugs. Of course. So we could sleep through the constant barrage of memories broadcast from the nearest jumbo screen. Yet again, Scott had focused on what would help keep us sane and moving. "Wyatt, leave me Dad's journal, would you?"

He hesitated, then whirled around. "Are you sure? Tonight? You really need sleep, Mom."

My heart ached for him. His concern was so sweet. "I'll try. But when I wake up, I want to see where we're headed. Plus, I need to mentally prepare for the procedures that we'll undergo."

He jerked his chin in response, looking very much like Scott. "Dad included a clipping on it. Extremely rare surgery. But apparently not as bad as it sounds."

I wondered how that could be…disengaging from a device embedded in one's brain for years. "See? You're ahead of me. Hand it over."

A ghost of a smile fell to his lips. "Okay. Sure." Wyatt dropped his bags, fished out the journal, and handed it off to me.

Grabbing the book, I gathered him into a hug. "One way or another, we're gonna be okay. I promise. Your dad believed it, and so do I."

Wyatt pulled away, studying my face, testing the strength of my words and conviction, I was sure. I could sense his brain racing into action as he yanked me back to him. "I'm worried about you, Mom. Well, both of us really. Don't check out again. Please."

I kissed his cheek. "Get some sleep and try not to worry. I'm here if you need anything."

He backed up, shouldered his bags, and headed toward the rear bedroom. "Night, Mom."

As nice as the thought of rest sounded, with Scott's research, my one lifeline to him at my fingertips, sleep wasn't happening tonight. Stopping off in the kitchen, I started some coffee, with no help from a digital assistant, since there didn't appear to be one, then scooted my bags into the bedroom next to me.

After filling my cup, I opened the leather journal, turning beyond the initial section to locate the information on the medical facility and our appointments scheduled for tomorrow. A map slid from the pages, and as I examined it closer, I found it to be a depiction of the area underground where the clinic must be.

The subway systems had been shut down over twenty years ago. Only the homeless and those involved in the illegal sale of goods proliferating among the maze of tunnels still existed down there.

Navigation would be difficult, no doubt. But I had to get a handle on it, since, from what I remembered Scott saying today, we would need to avoid detection of our noncompliance after the removal of our IC devices and travelling underground was the best way to accomplish that number one goal.

I spotted the facility on the map and traced backward to the safe house. The distance looked to be about one mile. But no telling what we might run into and what state the tunnels were in.

The summary Scott had included regarding the procedure offered just enough basic info, including risks to the patient and expected outcomes. The rest could wait. No other options existed at this point. This *was* the way forward, hazards and all.

The difficulties that lay ahead hit me like a brick wall as I tried to keep my rising dread from swallowing me whole. Wouldn't we always be fugitives within a world that thrived on being connected one hundred percent of the time, day and night? The inevitability of our capture, sooner or later, seemed unavoidable. *When* was the only question. Panic seized my thoughts, fear closing in, countered by one shaky breath in, then out. *Take it slow.* One day at a time. I talked myself down.

Keeping my mind busy turned out to be a good thing. The hours wore on. Reading details that Scott had gathered in such a short amount of time, evidence of how he had fought for our survival on every page, energised me, while I focused on what I could do and forced my mind away from the crushing loss I couldn't deal with, much less accept yet.

Flipping forward through the pages, I glanced over what else Scott had included. Earlier I hadn't given it much thought, but after the president's speech tonight, and hearing memories pouring from those monstrosities, I had to know more.

I navigated to the back, and an envelope slipped free. I grabbed it, read today's date in the corner and my name scribbled across the front in Scott's handwriting. Clutching the letter tightly, I snapped the journal closed, leaning against the headboard, my heart hammering in my chest.

No, no…NO… I screamed into the pillow, and it felt so liberating that I couldn't stop. I don't know how long I kept it up; until I fell asleep, I guess. Because hours later, splayed across the bed, exhausted, I woke to the sounds of more screaming. But not my own this time and not from a memory clamouring outside.

Wyatt

I stepped from the shower, the bit of routine echoing of the normalcy we'd left far behind today. After pulling on shorts, I stuck my head into the hallway, listening for Mom. Maybe she'd finally given in to sleep, but I doubted that, since I smelled coffee brewing. She was reading Dad's journal, which meant she'd find her own letter from him soon.

Mine was safely tucked away in my bag. But I couldn't make myself read it right now, knowing what was happening at home. Instead, my thoughts gravitated to the president's remarks we had heard tonight, all anticipated, thanks to Dad, but no less horrifying.

Unsurprisingly, the streets had emptied. After all, the man predicted the mysterious memory-wiping disease would spread, infecting the general population in record time, and that our best defence was, of course, quarantining ourselves. Tomorrow marked the beginning of the mandate for our collective isolation.

I threw open the window for a better view and fresh air. Our journey continued underground, starting in the morning, and that had me more than a little uneasy. Picturing the tight, cramped spaces had me gasping for breath already. I tried not to concentrate on what the next day would bring for me and Mom 'cause it's not like we had another option. We could die for having the devices removed; we could die on the table during surgery. We could be caught belowground and branded as traitors, dangerous to the masses—convicted of spreading the fake disease. Due to the widespread panic, insinuation held the same power as fact. Our lives were tenuous at best.

I found that freeing in a disturbing kind of way. Nothing guaranteed but the moment I existed within right now.

But the unsettling calm falling on the streets—after what we all heard tonight, what amounted to a death sentence sooner or later for all of us—had me shuddering. We'd been put on notice. Our leadership would do "all in our power for the people during these uncertain times." And in the interim, since public gatherings translated into greater risks for everyone, "Memorials would be held on the Jumbotrons, throughout the cities, so all could participate from the safety of their homes in the losses soon to come."

What a load of horseshit…using the same mechanism that had sunk the masses into darkness to remember them by. Meanwhile, they still lived, if you could call it that. Walking around in a haze, not aware of the past, present, or the ability to discern the future. Certainly appeared this administration had us all by the balls.

My gaze captured the tiny pockets of people here and there, scurrying from one place to the other, looking like bugs when caught in a bright ray of light. I could imagine their thoughts right now…their fears. For their families. For themselves. Not knowing what even tomorrow would bring. Their lives put on hold.

I cringed. The promise I'd made to my dad earlier today dug into my gut and embedded deeper, feeling like a lie.

His voice rang out in my head. "Get yourself safe first. Believe me. The time to fight will be here soon enough, and others—survivors like yourself—will join you. But you need to make it there, and that's a long road yet. Most won't, but you? You will, son."

I wished I had his confidence.

Mom and I had a leg up here, with Dad's grasp of the situation, but I still felt an overbearing doom pressing down on us. Like everyone else out there, I was prey, pure and simple, manoeuvring around their traps, waiting to be sniffed out and exposed.

I slid onto the window seat and pulled out my earplugs, startled to hear a young man about my age. The guy's name scrolled across the top of the feed. James… James Tucker. Engrossed, I watched as a younger version of him hit what was most likely the kid's first home run. The crowd went wild as he ran the bases. Next, a birthday celebration. Looked to be years later, but still a happy time. Next up a hockey game and a visit to the doc for stitches. His mouth had twisted in pain, but through it all, I could see his pride. His team must have won. Minutes after, the video winked out, and another took its place.

Glued to the screen, I waited for the next poor soul to snap to life before my eyes; as I did, my thoughts drifted to where the ill would be housed until they died, a mere shadow of their former selves.

Dad's journal had gone into some detail about the camps going up all over the city now and elsewhere. These facilities only got a mention in passing tonight. Understandably so, since the bigger shock wave at the moment had been the memory-altering "disease" that a whole generation of humans would face. Or better put—the systematic memory wipe underway.

Per Dad's documentation, these "hospitals" would be built to house thousands of people. Overflow areas were planned for outside, so that the sick could "enjoy nature." Conceptually, that didn't make sense. Could these individuals, emptied of themselves, actually enjoy anything?

How would they accommodate all those to come? Dad's writings hadn't mentioned that so far. Their numbers would continue to grow. Only those exempted from the beginning by design, along with however many existed, like us, would survive this memory culling. The blood iced in my veins. Dad didn't have time to get to this part yet. Most likely, the plan was still fluid. Already memorialised, dead in the eyes of the government, that just left the final step. What would prevent them from taking it?

A new branch of security had its inception today. Not peacekeepers or additional police force members, but those known as Collectors. This branch of the military, cue clanging bells in my head, would report directly to the president. Their job? To assimilate those who had succumbed but not reported to a housing facility. For the public good, all supposedly "infected" had to leave their families and be hospitalised. So we, the people, had been informed this evening.

This included planned door-to-door checks. Searches when the personnel deemed it necessary. Concern for public health demanded it, the president had spouted.

Compliance would be strictly enforced—for the good of all, of course.

Things were unfolding exactly as Dad had foretold. Didn't see any mention of these Collectors in his notes that I had read so far. Could have missed it. I needed another session with Dad's journal. Comforting, in a last-place sort of way, to know that Dad wouldn't be among those rounded up by this latest branch of the military.

My head lulled to the side, unable to keep my eyes from drifting shut. "No, no, no!" I shouted, alert again. I sat up straight, the silent blackness emanating from the Jumbotrons feeling odd. Bleary-eyed, I paused, hanging on to the emptiness. This newest form of media already felt like a drug, like what was engrained in our heads 24/7. We were born and bred for it. A perfect fit. Jesus, this was messed up.

As the feed initiated once more, I crashed the window shut and reached for my earplugs. Sighing out a long exhale, I felt the tension slide from my body. The best I could offer these people was to fight for the loved ones who still remained.

I crawled under the covers. "Lights off," I called out. An array of colours bloomed in my room. The Lost they were named in Dad's book, bled inside the walls, transmitting an eerie echo of their lives. Pulling a pillow over my head, I willed the darkness to take me under. Finally, the worst day of my life drew to an end.

Behind my eyelids, my dad wandered. I focused on his form, homed in on his stature. Any minute now, I'd free him from the prison that held him. I grabbed his arm. "Dad, it's me. Let's go. I'll take care of you. But hurry. They'll come for us."

Confusion flitted across his face, accentuated by eyes rounded with fear.

"Dad. It's Wyatt. Dad?"

"Help!" he screamed, then again, louder this time.

"Dad!" I gasped, as three men dragged me from my father. Tears streaked down his face, matching mine. "You don't belong here," I added, before my captors tossed me around the corner. A minute before a multitude of fists massaged my face.

I yelled, outraged, at my father, at myself, for getting caught, at the wrongness of the hand fate had dealt all of us.

"Son—wake up. Wyatt."

"Dad. Thank God. Dad… I've had a horrible nightmare." My mind reached out as I blinked awake into the harsh daylight, tiny shards of pain bursting alive in my head.

Mom yanked out my earplugs. "You were right on target, Wyatt." Her hand cupped my cheek. "Dad's gone, and the nightmare is still with us. Come here." She surrounded me in a hug. "You'll have to settle for me."

J.W. GARRETT

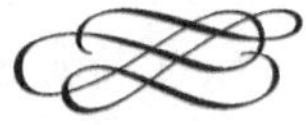

“I fixed us a big breakfast. Remember. After noon, you can’t eat or drink. Your procedure will be first. I’ll follow tomorrow morning.”

“I remember.”

“Do you want to talk about it?”

“Why? It won’t help. Dad will still be just as dead.”

“Right.” Wyatt put it all out there. The simple ugly truth. I didn’t know how to navigate these waters with my son, especially when my heart was bleeding from its own slow, but sure death wound. I lingered by the doorway, trying to think of something comforting. But the image Wyatt had conjured in my head had me clawing at the wall instead. The sorrow, the hurt, reflected in his eyes now shredded my insides. "I suspect our grief will be raw for a while. We've got each other. Let's cling to that."

"Yeah. Sure. Be right there."

Back in the kitchen, I filled our plates with eggs, sausage, and fruit, then poured coffee for both of us.

Five minutes later, Wyatt shuffled to the table and took a seat. "I won't ask how you slept. I heard you wake up off and on during the night. The walls are thin here," he added, shovelling in his first bite.

I shrugged. "Guilty as charged. I did get some reading done from the journal, though. I think I have a better handle on where we're going."

"Aren't you concerned about ditching our car? Heading out on foot, for what? The duration?"

"I am. But your dad had planned for us to sell it underground, in the Nest. That's what it's called. We'll need the money to survive without our devices to conduct transactions."

Wyatt huffed a laugh at me. "I know what it's called, Mom. And I'm more than a little sceptical that this part of Dad's plan will work out at all. I mean, actual cash for stuff? I don't even remember the last time I touched paper money. Besides today, rummaging around in my bag. I find it hard to accept people use the stuff. It's archaic."

"Can't say I'm looking forward to this, uh, journey myself, but I believe what your dad had to say. So we'll trust in his plan." Wyatt gave a solemn nod, then took his last bite. "More?"

"Nah. I'm good."

"Wyatt, I've been thinking… How would you feel about us having our own…memorial for Dad?" I tossed a glance his way, tentatively gauging his reaction.

"Here? Now?" His gaze travelled to the tiny kitchen.

"Yeah. That was my thought. It's just us. Doesn't need to be fancy. Or long. I feel like it would help me. Maybe."

His expression flashed confusion, before tears pooled in his eyes, like holding back a dam.

"I get it." I gripped his hand as he hung his head. *Help him through it. He'll need your strength.* Scott's voice rang out in my mind.

"We're gonna be all right. Eventually."

Wyatt sniffled, giving me a clipped nod.

"Let's both choose our favourite vacation the three of us took together, share some memories. Your dad loved our time as a family, away from the day-to-day stresses of life."

"Okay. I'm game." Wyatt met my gaze, a spark of amusement in his eyes. "Real or simulated?"

"Real. On the count of three, let's send our answers to each other."

"This is the last time we can do something like that, before our devices end up on a junk heap."

"True… One, two, three, go!"

"I don't believe you, Mom… You didn't like camping in the Smoky Mountains, especially the fishing part," he scoffed.

"False. Just not for the same reasons you did."

"Let's hear it then—the rest of the story." He leaned in closer and grinned.

I'd been honest, but I couldn't give him the entire truth—that, when Wyatt was proudly cooking his catch, and Scott and I had taken a walk, we'd had a passionate lovemaking session in the woods. I felt my cheeks heating and redirected my thoughts as I refilled my cup.

"Sure. Here goes…" I lowered to my seat, downing a large swallow of coffee. "While I don't personally enjoy fishing, I savoured the quiet time to take in the scenery, walk among nature, hike, read, and, of course, our nightly campfires."

"Okay…" Wyatt hit me with a challenging stare. "I'll buy that. For me, it was coming back with a bigger catch than Dad, for the first time ever. And you getting Dad to sing at night by the campfire. Dad seemed happy, relaxed. He didn't let loose very often," Wyatt said, as a melancholy look washed over his face. "But he did that trip."

"He sure did," I couldn't help adding.

"Then when we dragged that old-fashioned rowboat out on the lake—"

"A very bad idea. I warned you both. Remember?"

"You suck at rowing, Mom. We finally found something you're not good at."

I shrugged. "We made it back, didn't we?"

"With one oar. And it took forever."

I rolled my eyes. "All part of the fun."

Twenty minutes later, both of us crying from laughing so hard, I ended, totally spontaneously, by reciting Scott's favourite poem, *The Road Not Taken.* When I got to the end of the first stanza, I hadn't expected that Wyatt would pick up the second. I recited the third, and he finished with the last.

Wyatt scooted from the table and reached out for me, tears spilling down his cheeks. Silently, we rocked back and forth, giving him the opportunity to get out some of his grief. When Wyatt stilled, I pulled away and lifted my gaze to his. "Thank you, Wyatt."

"He was everything to me, Mom."

"I know, son. Me too. But we'll make it through. I can feel him with us."

Wyatt wiped his nose against his sleeve. "I think so too. And, Mom?"

"Yeah?"

"This was one of your better ideas."

I kissed his forehead. "Occasionally I hit the mark."

Wyatt gifted me with a smile through his watery gaze, then gathered the plates, and we cleaned the kitchen accompanied by the tune of clattering dishes and the repetitive drone of memories in the background.

"Okay." I took a deep breath and exhaled slow. "It's time. Gather your things, and we'll get moving, after I add to our supplies from the kitchen staples in here."

Thirty minutes later, Wyatt, taking point, poring over the hand-drawn map, we ambled toward the closest entrance to the Nest. My fears about carrying two bags for the duration turned out to be well-founded. One of the bags I'd secured to my back. The other single-strapped one I'd slung across my chest, the bag resting at hip level. It'd do for now. Considering parting with anything among the items Scott and I had carefully chosen wasn't an option.

"I think this is it." Wyatt's gaze travelled the length of the battered door. "I thought we might have to face a security scan here."

"*Hmm.* Maybe not. I'll take another look at Dad's notes. Keep in mind these subway routes were shut down before the advent of the cutting-edge IC devices in use today and before the advancements in security tech in place now too. Getting inside may be easier than you think."

I'd already read the instructions for today's travel. Nothing about access to the underground, so I flipped further back in Scott's notebook and noticed a section labelled Additional Information, then scrolling down the page, the heading: passwords. "Ah. I think I found something. There should be a keypad."

"How quaint. Yeah, I found it."

"Looks like there is a system of rotating passwords here. Try this—241581."

The door clicked open. "Old school… Nice. We're in." Wyatt grunted a laugh. "Good going, Mom. Come on."

"Wait. Get your flashlight." I dug into my side pocket, scrounging for mine.

His brief yell echoed before a resounding *thud.* "Ugh… Shit."

I flashed my light down to his prone form. "Are you okay?"

"I think so. I fell on top of one of my bags. Toss yours to me, then grab those iron rungs and work your way down."

"Not so bad." I joked with him just a little, evaluating the distance. "Don't always be in such a hurry. About five feet. Give or take. But who knows next time?"

He shook out his arms and legs and resettled the straps of his gear. "Everything appears to still be working. Come on, light up ahead."

Water splashed under my boots as I took up my flashlight, shining the beam around me for a better view. The place smelled musty, stale, and damp, with the heavy scent of chemicals permeating the air. We walked along a raised platform; to the far right, I spied tracks and the old subway cars. And higher up, a huge piece of signage hung, precariously attached; in fact, it looked as if it might fall at any minute. The portion remaining read only *Station.*

Pieces of history that I ached to explore—all of it. Now wasn't the time though. Here and there, rotted suitcases dotted our path, like the occupants had been forced to abandon them in the face of some higher or more immediate purpose. What must those of that generation been facing? Maybe another day I could gather additional clues. Find out more about the people who carried those burdens. I felt an unusual bond with their circumstances, considering the way my life had suddenly veered off course.

"About two-tenths more," I shouted out to Wyatt up ahead.

"Yeah, I hear voices." He slowed, waiting for me. And as we rounded the next corner, his words mirrored my thoughts. "I think we've found the Nest."

We shared a glance, navigating throughout the diverse groups. At first, I had been concerned we might not fit in among this crowd…carting our baggage, our clothing evidence of our travels, a mother and her son. But it became quickly apparent that an eclectic mix of people added to the unique atmosphere of the place.

Merchants haggled for everything from food and clothing to equipment parts and specialised medical devices. Animated voices reached agreement, then fists pumped the air, cash raised high, exchanging hands in the process. And tobacco… I sniffed. Treated as contraband above, it had evidently found a home and was alive and well down here too. I breathed in the scent and held it. God, how long had it been? Down here I could have a cigarette again, but I won't… I won't. One slow exhale later had me reconsidering.

"Mom…where has this place been all my life?" Wyatt's mouth hung open, eyes wide, eagerly working to digest the sights before us.

"Safely out of your reach."

We'd found a stretch of ground where time stood still. And this was *the* Nest. Raw energy crackled through the space. Small tightly knit groupings in the crowd screamed over others, desperate to get their point across, or maybe, their point across first? Emotions scrolled over faces as individuals vied for the same item—angst, desperation, anger, then finally victory or defeat.

Whoops and high fives ensued in quick celebration, as the sought-after items changed hands. But that look of pure satisfaction, rare in our world these days, appeared to be its own reward. The last time I'd experienced this much intensity and excitement in one space had been… Well, never. Somehow, it all worked in a very engaging fashion. I could easily get addicted to the vitality and power pulsing through this place.

No one even noticed as we passed through the main drag. I took a closer look. The underground economy was booming. "Unbelievable…" I slowed, making mental notes along the way, relieved that an abundance of people down here transacted their business in cold, hard cash.

Ahead, Wyatt hesitated, then turned and immersed himself with a merchant, his head bent in conversation with a young woman. Sixteen maybe, I'd guess. By the time I reached the pair, Wyatt smirked proudly and handed over a hardback book to the girl—a real book.

"Wyatt?"

"Mom. This is…"

"Oh, sorry." The girl flashed a pretty smile, clearly for my son's benefit. "I'm Tess."

"Wyatt, and this is my mom, Ellie."

"Nice to meet you all. I'm no good at bartering. That man was about to take advantage of me. Your son saved me five bucks."

Wyatt played shy as crimson rose to his cheeks. "Happy to help. And nice to meet you." Then he lifted his chin ahead, down another brightly lit corridor. "I think this way, Mom."

Tess's eyes brightened. "Oh. I'm heading that way too."

"Feel free to come along. But our stop isn't far," Wyatt said. "I wish you well. Enjoy *Moby Dick*."

Her head bowed as she clutched the book close to her chest. "It was my dad's favourite. I would have paid even more than that man had asked of me," she mumbled, her voice quieting.

"Here we are, Wyatt," I announced, breaking the

awkward silence hovering between them, swinging my gaze back to the girl, then to my son, in a do-something plea.

Tess's eyes widened in recognition. "Dr Savin," she read aloud from the nameplate. "This is my stop too."

I gave Wyatt a nod. He shrugged, turning the knob, and pushed open the door to the sound of its squeaky complaint. My heart sank, my fingers working through Scott's notes. "Yep, this is it."

I took a step inside, kicking up dust and almost stumbling into a bookcase in the centre of the room's clutter. My eyes adjusting quickly, I reached for my flashlight and flicked the beam along the perimeter of the space. At our feet, a path trailed through the dust. "Look." I waved Wyatt to me, and we snaked our way around the mess. Straight ahead was another door, off in the corner of the room, a crack of light lining its base.

"Good eye, Mom." Wyatt gave me a broad smile. "This might be it." He moved to shove it open.

"No, let me." Grabbing the gun from my waistband, I motioned Wyatt and Tess backward, Wyatt groaning in protest. "*Shh*," I hissed, raising my weapon, inching slowly ahead.

8

Wyatt

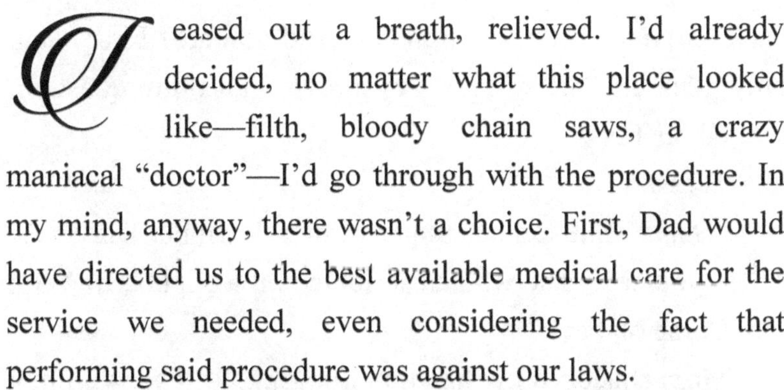

I eased out a breath, relieved. I'd already decided, no matter what this place looked like—filth, bloody chain saws, a crazy maniacal "doctor"—I'd go through with the procedure. In my mind, anyway, there wasn't a choice. First, Dad would have directed us to the best available medical care for the service we needed, even considering the fact that performing said procedure was against our laws.

Second, given the momentous events taking place in our world, I had to be prepared to survive. This was the way. Third, I wouldn't let Dad's sacrifice for us mean nothing. At the end of the day, when the dust settled, not many would be walking around with all their marbles intact. I planned to be one of them, one of the Unfound, fighting for myself and in memory of those who could not.

Nosing into the room, I drew a deep breath. Another good sign, disinfectant—that sterile hospital smell, but here, well, maybe I'd not die of infection at least.

"Thank God," Mom murmured, before tucking away her piece. She and a lady spoke near a tiny window up front, before Mom waved me closer.

"Wyatt," the lady behind the window beamed a trained smile at me. "Right on time. We need to get you back and prepped to take a few pictures."

"I'm coming with him," Mom interjected.

I didn't mess with Mom when she looked like that. This lady didn't either.

"Of course, after we get him set up, you can come back. Give us just a few minutes. And you are? First name only, please." The woman's eyebrows shot up in question, riveted on Tess.

"Tess."

"*Hmm.*" She ran her finger further down her list. "Yes. There you are." The woman scribbled on a clipboard. "You too. Come on back."

Mom squeezed my hand, murmuring, "I'll see you in a few."

I knew that was true. Mom wouldn't let some lady with a clipboard stand between us. I followed her down a series of hallways. Tess and I were separated, and after a set of x-rays, I was left in a room, instructed to undress, and don a hospital gown.

Then I waited, reading the posters on the walls about diseases that could be eradicated with an injection, and pregnancy prevention, but nothing about carving out IC devices. Probably too much to cover with a poster blurb. Now that I was here though, the thought of yanking out a piece of technology that had been sewn inside my head seventeen years ago, embedded within everything up there that made me, *me*, sent an icy shiver down my spine.

The door opened with the characteristic whir of a cyborg being announcing its presence. Following it, a man with salt-and-pepper hair entered and closed the door.

His age meant he'd be more experienced at this, right?

"Pardon the intrusion. A few more diagnostics, then we'll invite your mother back before she blows up the place, trying to get to you."

"Sounds like Mom. I'd watch my step around her if I were you."

He chuckled, then turned loose the automaton to his duties. "I don't anticipate any problems. You're young, and your brain tissue will heal, but it's unlikely your brain will function properly with another IC device, should you decide to input one again later." The doctor directed a knowing glance toward me. "I'm obligated to mention that."

"Thank you, but I don't think I'll need another."

He crossed his arms over his chest and rocked on his heels. "If you're caught, you'll be forced to take one."

"Then I'll have to take my chances."

"Let me be frank."

"Please do."

"I know your father very well. We'll need good men on the other side of this. Those he has sent my way are the best of the best. It's my hope, with their help, they'll lead us out of this horror."

I slowly scrutinised him. Dad always said a man speaks in many ways and usually tells you everything you need to know about him with his body language alone, if you're perceptive and patient enough. No words necessary. I nodded, satisfied, but still unwilling to give up any details my dad had shared in his journal—his words—intended only for us.

I did learn something new. Mulling over what the doc had told me, I categorised it away. Evidently, Dad had saved more people than just us. Comforting, since the zombielike creatures above seemed to multiply by the hour. Assuming I came outta this in one piece, we needed to find these "others" and band together 'cause the world was falling apart around us, and I had faith the people Dad had helped could be instrumental in finding a new way of things.

The cyborg communicated its findings, while I watched the interaction between it and the doc, ascertaining what little I could about my fate.

"All appears to be in order," Doc said. "I'll send in your mother, and we'll administer a sedative."

"Great." A nervous smile worked across my mouth. "How long will it take?"

"Two hours, minimum, could take up to six or longer. Everyone's different. Depends on your body's reactions. We'll let you set the pace as we move through. Don't want you to lose any brain functionality along the way."

"I'm with you there."

Mom breezed into the room. "Everything okay in here?"

"Fine, just fine," the doc assured both of us. "I'll send in the nurse."

"Wyatt, how ya doing?"

Mom's gaze hit me hard, and I wondered, not for the first time, how the mom gene could hit so succinctly in equal doses of love and compliance. "I'm good."

"I'll be here. So you can relax."

"Thanks, Mom. Will you also check in on Tess? I don't think she has anyone. She's bound to be scared."

"Sure, I will."

A few minutes later, sedative on board, I mumbled words meant to be a comfort to my mom, but only a slurred tangle of syllables slipped from my mouth.

"See you on the other side, Wyatt."

A veil crept over my eyes. The last thought that fluttered through me was a blissful sweet surrender, and I welcomed it as it took possession and swept me under.

A cool hand brushed my forehead, then slid to my cheek.

"Wyatt. Wake up, honey. Show us you can speak."

A fog thickened my thoughts, everything inside my head like a slow-moving mound of molasses. *I hear you*, I wanted to say. But words wouldn't come. Something in there was up to speed though…Claws of fear inched their way through me, their power paralysing, or maybe I actually was. If this were all that remained of me, then I'd let go. Dad waited on the other side. I was confident. Ready even. His voice rang in my ears, but before I could answer, I collapsed back into a dark miasma of nothingness.

"Wyatt. Wake up!"

"Okay, okay. Stop screaming. My head feels like a battle zone." I blinked, opening my eyes to Mom's fearful, worried face. I felt bad when I made her do that.

"Thank God, Wyatt." Mom pressed a kiss to my forehead. "You had me scared to death. How do you feel?"

"Hungry." I stared at the tubes running from my arms. Recognition dawning, I reached for my head, meeting bandages. "Well…am I still in one piece?"

"Doc said you threw them a few curve balls, but the

procedure went well."

"Good. So you'll go tomorrow."

"Hoping to, but Wyatt, you've been out of it for three days. I'll wait a little longer if necessary."

"Three days? Yeah. I feel okay. I think. Don't wait any longer, Mom, please. Get that thing outta you. Promise me. Tomorrow."

"I'll give you a tentative yes." Her hand moved to my forehead; cool, comforting. My eyelids fought to stay open. "Food's on the way. How does it feel inside?"

"Quiet," I mouthed out, reaching for the old automatic connection. "Empty."

The door whooshed open. "He's out of the woods," Doc stated. "I'm sure you're not surprised to hear he's got a very strong will."

"Not in the least. He comes by that honestly."

No truer words were ever spoken. I got a double dose of that from the maker, no doubt. A heaviness fell over me, and my eyelids drifted shut.

9

Wyatt

Now it was Mom's turn and being on the other end of this coin was crap. She'd come out of surgery but hadn't woken yet. Between worrying about her and Tess, who was roaming around somewhere, just out of bed, I paced back and forth, trying to concentrate instead on Dad's theorics of the endgame here.

No use. Besides, this stuff in Dad's journal… It was *way* out there… Beings from who-the-hell-knew-where. Summoned? Helped along, drawn by the continuously piping memories, like its own personal calling card, sounded like. I'd read about it twice already, thinking I'd misinterpreted it. Or maybe it was coded, and I didn't have the key. Either way, I needed a break.

Massaging my forehead, I muttered a curse, closed the journal, and left it by Mom's bed. Her stats and heart rate were good. An hour ago, when the doc had checked in, he'd smiled and said Mom came out of surgery in better condition than I had. Dad always said she had strength enough for the three of us.

I poked my head into the hallway; looked like their skeleton crew was stretched way too thin. Business had picked up too. Out of rote habit, I dipped into my IC device to send a quick message to Mom. Throwing my hands in the air, I growled and grabbed a slip of paper and pen, scribbled a note for her, at the last minute adding the date and time and a smiley face. Weird for me, but it was Mom.

Damn, this would take some getting used to. Sending a message through my device took mere seconds, like a thought. Now? Searching for paper, pen, writing… I'd spent four or five minutes, and she might not find the stupid thing. I shoved the torn scrap of paper in Dad's journal, half of it hanging out. Surely she would see that.

I passed by Tess's room once more. Still empty. She could be anywhere around the place. I combed the halls, not really believing she was here, then took off for the Nest. I barely knew Tess, but I did have some idea what was running through her newly emptied brain at the moment. I was in a fog for days afterward. Might be she's reaching for help, mixed up and counting on an apparatus no longer in place. I felt for her plight. She had no one down here.

Pushing my way through the busy crowd roving the Nest, I glanced left, right, scouring the stalls set up, homing in on the individual people milling around. Blonde hair, blue eyes, average height, wearing who-knows-what… She'd be easy to spot among the grungy riffraff. I shuffled through the entirety of the space, hoping for a glimpse, but nothing.

What were my thoughts when I came to a few days ago? Mostly a mangled mess of who-the-hell-knew-what. I remembered that first primal instinct I had, though. Escape… The need to run. With only what my pockets could hold 'cause I shouldn't be gone long, I headed out. My mom needed me for once, so I committed to finding Tess and returning in a few hours' time. But her situation could be much more dire than I'd originally thought, if she made it street side.

I retraced our steps the way we entered down here, almost a week ago now, weaving in and out among the people busy making deals, transacting their business for the day. The energy of the tribe gathering in this subterranean place pulsed through my veins, calling me back as I shuffled my way through.

Soon… What an odd kinship. I didn't know these people, yet. We did have one trait in common. Outlaws. All of us. And that bound us into a unique tribe. What was once deemed a deficiency…a curse, was now a blessing; we lived unconnected and virtually unseen. The Unfound.

I reached the spot where we'd literally fallen underground and scaled the metal ladder to the surface. Pushing my weight on the door, it gave way easily, swinging wide, while I slipped outside. It clicked closed again, and muttering a reminder under my breath, I made a mental note, since I couldn't make a real note, of the password to gain entrance, hoping I'd remembered it correctly and that it hadn't cycled to another.

I peered into the night. Regret threatening to pull me back below. This might have been really stupid. Separating myself from Mom this way to help someone who was little more than a stranger. So much could go wrong in an instant. In my heart, though, I felt Dad would approve, and that seemed to be my bar now. The repetitive thrum from the latest wave of memories hit me as I scrambled to my feet.

Streetlamps splashed the evening with points of light, intermittently breaking up the gathering gloom. Small rings of people bustled about, moving along at a steady pace, not lingering anywhere too long.

I scanned the street, looking for anyone out of place, determined to give myself an hour, two max, before heading back to Mom. At least then I'd know I tried. Off in the distance, at the next corner, a girl paused. Silhouetted against the glow from the nearest light, I could make out her flowy white hospital gown. God, this was bad. If she were out of her mind enough to get here, how would I lead her underground without causing a scene?

I hurried to intercept her as she crossed into the street. Lights highlighted her startled face.

Four men coming from the opposite direction, inching their way forward, beat me to Tess.

Shit. I planted myself against the brick wall. So close. I'd almost made it to her.

"Look at her," one yelled. "She doesn't even know where the hell she is. We've caught ourselves another," he taunted.

In a last-ditch effort, she pitched backward and wheeled around, but her body movements jerked wildly, her arms flailing. The effects of the anaesthesia still coursed through her system. Her half-hearted attempt to outrun the men pulled them out into full view, bathing them in the streetlamp's stark light.

I peeled myself from the building, straining to see. "Collectors… Damn it!"

"Let's see what we got here," a fat man snickered, while the three remaining men circled Tess.

"She's done for. Just look in her eyes. Nobody's home," a second man added.

"What's your name, kid?" the third asked.

"It's, uh, Te…" she stammered.

"Uh-huh. Do you live around here? Address?"

I crawled closer, now able to see her blank stare.

"Mother's name, father's name," the man asked. "Well, missed each one. Let's get you put away before you hurt yourself. You're in luck," he sneered. "Our newest holding area is only a block down the road." Snatching her arms, the small posse led her away.

A questionnaire…a test of some sort. One that she failed.

I followed until the bright stadium lights cast a spotlight on the facility for the Lost. That went up quick. Less than a week ago, that piece of land had been a park. I swivelled, backtracked to my underground location, keyed in the password, which thankfully still worked, and lowered myself inside.

Once below, I manoeuvred back to the merchant who I'd dealt with before. Luckily, the man carried an inventory of more than just books. Maybe he'd recall our previous dealing, might even give me a break this time.

The clothing options weren't numerous, but I appeared too tidy, as is. I needed a quick judgment, like they'd doled out to Tess.

"See something that strikes your fancy?"

I tilted my head side to side. "Somewhat."

A glint of recognition lit his gaze. "You again." He

craned his neck and puffed smoke from the cigar plugging his face. "No pretty girl with you this time, eh?"

"Not this time. I need to look like you," I announced, taking a side glimpse of his offerings. "Do you have some clothes I can trade for?"

"You want to look like me?"

"Right. Quickly. I don't have a lot of time."

"Yeah. If I could sell chunks of time, I'd not be haggling down here."

"Wouldn't that be something? Yes or no. Can you help me?"

He gazed at me from top to bottom, then nodded. "I believe so. Follow me."

Minutes later, assessing my choice in a full-length mirror, I muttered, "This will do." I'd traded a new cable sweater for what amounted to little more than rags. The man had made a sweet deal, but I got what I need from the exchange. "I'll see you around."

"Anytime." He coughed and spit in a can at his feet. "I'm here for whatever you need."

After a quick stop to check on Mom and drop off my ID and the clothing I didn't lose to the trade I'd just made, I retraced my steps, then slowed and loitered beyond the fenced-in holding area.

My ID would surely give me away, but so would a routine scan, confirming my lack of necessary IC equipment. Either of those options could be the end of me.

Instead, counting on the laziness of the Collectors I'd seen in action, I'd bet on being thrown inside based on a superficial evaluation alone. Like Tess. A mixture of anxiety and fear rippled through me as I wondered how long it'd be before more Collectors would show their faces.

As fate would have it, not long at all.

The same four men rounded a corner, striding confidently my way. I shambled ahead, gaze fixed at the nothingness above their heads.

"You there."

I kept walking.

"Stop. Now."

I still kept walking.

The man stepped in my path. "Name." He spat out.

"Uh. Name…" I repeated, my voice monotone.

"Address."

I stared forward. Mute.

"Like damn cattle. All of them. *Moo*," he added, barking a laugh.

My fist clenched, straining against my barely bridled need to punch him in the face.

"You're at the right place. Come on. Move it." They boxed me in, guiding me between the gates, then retreated, and with a final squeak of metal, slammed them shut again. I kept my movements slow, trying not to react, gazing at the hundreds contained in this small space. Tess would probably gravitate toward the perimeter. That was my first instinct.

I scanned the people roaming the periphery, my gaze lighting on their terror-filled faces. And sure enough, off to the far right, I spotted her, Tess, her white gown smeared in mud, where she huddled near a tree.

10

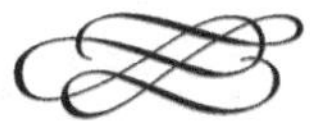

My eyes opened to a murky blur. “Where am I? God, I hurt all over.” Focusing my gaze, I homed in on images. A chair, a bright light… “Doctor?”

“Yes, yes. It’s me.”

I lifted a hand to my head, meeting bandages, entwining myself in tubes. “I remember. How’d it go?”

“The procedure went well. No major complications to speak of. But it’ll take you a few days to be up and around. I insist you take it easy. I’ll drug you if I have to.”

"Why the hard sell? I'll listen. You've given me no reason not to trust you. Just give me water. Please."

He gave me a placating smile and called over his assistant. "Coming right up."

I gulped down large swallows, eyeing the man. "What is it? I'm a mom. I can practically read minds."

His lips thinned to a straight line. "It's Wyatt and Tess. They're gone."

I jerked up to a sit. "Oh no…" I reached out to steady myself. "Maybe I shouldn't have done that."

Doc eased me back down. "No, you shouldn't. Try something like that again, and I'll sedate you. Your insides need time to heal. Period."

"Got it."

"I don't want to upset you further. I'll move along so you can rest."

"No, don't go. Tell me what you know. I'll be still and just listen. I promise." The man had more information about my son, damn it! I schooled my face to a calm, passive demeanour. The opposite of what smouldered inside me.

He stared at me, evaluating. "All right," he agreed, his brows knotting.

"Mind telling me your real name? I guess I could keep calling you Doc, if you'd prefer."

"Charlie." He lowered to a round stool. "I don't mind at all."

"Okay. Let me have it."

He blew out a breath. "Well, your son left shortly after you came out of surgery. Your stats had stabilised. Although nothing's for certain in cases like these, we'd confirmed for him that you were basically out of the woods."

"Was there a problem during Tess's surgery? Or, uh, I don't know…maybe you can't tell me that information."

"I've crossed so many lines already, helping others like you, for instance. I just let my conscience guide me now. I pick and choose my battles, doing what's right for as long as I can." He ticked his head to the side and shrugged. "When I can't, I guess they'll have me."

I scrutinised his body language. "They?"

Doc began again, ignoring my question. "Her procedure went as expected. But she woke up, took out her lines, and bailed. Kids have more energy, even after surgery like this. I'm concerned she'll have bleeding in her brain if she's not taking it easy, wherever she is."

"I see."

"My guess is your son went after her."

I sighed, the noise leaving me in a growl. "Sounds like something he'd do."

"I hope he brings her back soon." Doc must have caught the look in my eyes. Wagging his finger back and forth, he spouted, "Don't even think about it, Ellie. In a day or so, you can go above and search for him, assuming all proceeds well on this end."

"Okay, what do you need me to do to show you I'm all right?"

A lopsided grin crossed his mouth. "Let's start with broth, shall we, then work our way up from there?"

With a pat on my arm, Doc Charlie left. And bound and determined to be set free, I resigned myself to his regimen for the moment, all the while wishing my son through my door.

The soup was delicious. After a second helping, my energy returning, I made the necessary rounds to the bathroom, then slowly wandered the floor. I counted ten patients currently in various stages of recovery under Doc Charlie's care. By day two, up and about, I had the space almost entirely mapped out, except for one closed-off corridor I had yet to explore.

Why I thought it mysterious or why my steps slowed as I neared the lone door, I'm not sure. Maybe because only one of them was located down this long expanse? Or the hair rising along my skin. Odd… My hand hovered over the doorknob, listening for voices…sounds of life…anything that would give me an idea of what I might encounter enclosed behind the wall. On the other side, the mechanical whir of machinery hissed and sputtered in a continual pattering and smacking of gears.

More patients? Something darker, more ominous perhaps? Resolute, I twisted the knob and pushed inside.

Rows and rows of beds confronted me. Weaving in and out among them, several cyborgs trolled back and forth, attending efficiently to patients who appeared nonresponsive. No one seemed alarmed by my presence in this quiet space, though, so I stepped deeper into the room.

One thing they all had in common: age. These people were old. Immobile. And they didn't appear conscious. A death cloud hung over the lot of them, as if they were one foot in the grave already. The putrid odour of ruined flesh reached my nose, chased by a whiff of disinfectant. My skin crawled as I fought the urge to run. The end felt close here. Like it was comfortable, biding its time, confident of imminent success. Sorting this out later seemed a better idea. Being here was…overpowering.

I turned. Doc Charlie darkened the doorway. "What is this place?" I asked, the words rushing from my mouth in a gush of breath.

He led me into the hallway and guided me to a chair. "Very important work." He raised an eyebrow. "Thought you might already have an inkling."

"Why on Earth would you think such a thing?"

"Because of your husband's involvement."

My gaze shot to his. "I guess you should know…since you two were connected. I sense he trusted you, or he wouldn't have entrusted us to your care." I took a deep breath, preparing to say out loud what I'd been avoiding. "He's gone. Scott is…dead."

"I'm sorry to hear that, Ellie." Charlie squeezed my shoulder. "Can't say I'm surprised, though. I've never met a man more committed to working toward the common good. It's because of Scott that we have the beginnings of a bare bones plan at all."

"What do you mean? I don't follow."

"Maybe I've said too much."

"Ah, no you don't. Spill it."

Charlie bowed his head and nodded, like he was affirming the words before he set them free. "Scott mentioned to those of us who worked closely with him that soon he'd be documenting his plans and sharing them in some format with you and Wyatt. What's coming for us is big, Ellie."

"He documented it. But I haven't opened his journal in days. Due to the surgery, and, well, it's hard to think about. It's easier not to, I'll admit." I blinked back the tears prickling my eyes. "Some days I feel as if I might shatter into a million pieces, and I think, if I hold my breath, muscle through, I'll keep it all together."

"Ellie, I understand." He patted my hand. "Believe me. I do. But this encompasses more than you, Wyatt, and Scott's team at work."

"I do know that much."

"Go and catch up. Read. You're sidelined for a little longer anyway." Doc crooked his thumb toward the room full of old people. "And then we'll talk again about why those patients behind that door there are so important."

"Okay. I will."

On the way back to my room, thoughts of Scott in the middle of some master plot against our government sparked to life in my head. Doc was right; my usefulness was limited without fully accessing the resources Scott gave me. Entrusted to me. He didn't just leave a map toward safety, apparently it was a design for so much more.

When I dropped into a chair and opened Scott's journal, a piece of paper floated from the pages. Snatching it from the air, I quickly scanned Wyatt's note, left over a day ago. Just as I'd suspected, he'd gone in search of Tess. Stronger, steadier now, I'd head out tonight, with or without Doc's blessing. But first, with the help of Scott's writings, I'd fit at least one of the missing pieces of this jumbled puzzle into place before leaving.

Buried in Scott's words, the deeper I got, the harder it was to stop. A soul-piercing fear licked up my spine. Oh my God. How could this be true? And if all this were true, how would we ever survive it? A knock cut through my thoughts. "Come in."

"Thought you might be dug in by now." Charlie laid a tray of food on the nightstand.

"Room service? Thanks. But I can get around. And, like it or not, I'll be leaving to find my son tonight."

"I figured as much. I could tell by the light in your eyes. But eat first, then I'll fill in what I can. Let me warn you. Keep an open mind."

"*Mmm-hmm*," I hummed, grabbing a roll, as I glanced up, then ducked back into my reading.

11

I took in my surroundings, stifling my gag reflex as the overwhelming stench hit me. The crowd moved aimlessly, not headed anywhere in particular, slowly shuffling one foot in front of the other. An emptiness swept through me. The term *Lost* made perfect sense in this horrific place. I shuddered, confronted with the reality of our lives now. All these people—never to know their family again or understand what made them who they are—were…my new reality.

Here and there, nowhere designated, they stooped and

relieved themselves, not appearing to care about others passing or gathered beside them. I lifted my shirt over my nose, blocking some of the odour, but the nastiness was pervasive and the conditions barbaric. How would they live like this? Too many people clustered together with no thought given to their well-being. Swallowing hard, I tried to keep the meagre contents of my stomach from making a reappearance.

Worming my way through the crowds, gingerly stepping around the filth, I attempted to avoid the larger hordes. They wouldn't move to allow my passage, as I'd expected, though. Instead, they'd stare into my eyes with their hollow gazes, faces smeared with layers of muck, somehow communicating a yearning so powerful that I found it difficult to tear my gaze away, drawn in deeper by the pleading they silently conveyed.

This could have been me…

Raw emotions churned in my gut as I switched up my tactic. Focused on the ground, I picked out a path to Tess. Every few feet I'd glance up, check that she hadn't moved, then continue on my way. I let out a relieved sigh, making it within arm's reach of her, and extended my hand. "Tess? Are you okay?"

She jerked and manoeuvred further away from me.

"It's Wyatt."

This time she took a good look, tilting her head, studying me, her eyes swimming with tears. "Wyatt?"

I nodded and folded her trembling body into a hug.

"Something's not right. In my head. I tried to get help. But something's wrong with everyone here. No one will listen to me. I'm not sure how I ended up in this place. How did I get here? Do you know?"

Her eyes, full of confusion, met mine, but I just held her until her shaking stopped. Wishing I still had my heavier sweater, I yanked off my outer layer and wrapped her inside. "That doesn't matter." We rocked back and forth until the tension eased from her shoulders. "We need to get you outta here and to the Doc. That's what is most important now. He can help you."

"Doc?" Recognition dawned on her face.

"Thank God. You remember."

"Yes. Some, I think. But my memories feel jumbled… Out of order." Blood slid down Tess's neck, oozing from her ear.

I shuffled through the warning signs as they popped in my head. The ones Doc had mentioned before surgery—brain bleeds and memory loss were top of the list. My concern for her kicked up several notches. "Let's sit down for a few minutes." I settled her to the ground and nestled close, attempting to share my body heat.

Tess required treatment. We needed to get the hell outta here. Escape was our only option. I identified potential weaknesses along the pen holding us in. The structure didn't appear like it could withstand an assault, but plenty of Collectors patrolled the perimeter, guns by their side, more than making up for that fact.

Huge lamps flickered on overhead, dousing the entire yard in blinding light. Collectively, the crowd shied back, shielding their eyes, while they gasped and groaned. On the far end of our makeshift cage, Collectors corralled the people forward, funnelling them toward what looked to be a sorting station, maybe the point where they'd initially scan their IC devices for personal data.

I'd expected this… Shit. This was bad…really bad. We needed to be gone before they got to us.

"Hey." I squeezed her hand, pulling Tess's attention from the commotion mounting around us. "Tell me something you remember, about a place or a time when you felt safe."

Her eyes transformed, the turmoil swirling there clearing, until they held a calming light. "Home," she began, "before this nightmare started."

"Tell me about it."

She nodded. "Okay, maybe just a little. My parents are doctors. They're always busy, but when one is at the hospital, the other is off, so it works. We do everything together. We were even remodelling our home." She flashed me a smile, odd with the ongoing commotion, but that didn't matter. Whatever it took to keep her mind busy. "That's what I'm studying—interior design. They were my first clients."

"I see. Why didn't they come with you? Have the procedure done themselves?"

"They sent me on ahead." Her voice shook. "They were supposed to be coming a few hours behind me. Said choosing what to pack might take a little while."

"Guess they realised the surgery was a necessity," I added, trying to keep her talking.

"Yes. They knew Doc from somewhere."

All around us, scuffling and isolated fighting escalated, becoming more intense. Tess didn't seem to notice, tucked away in her own world, but icy fingers of panic slithered through me, gripping me tight. Doubtful I could protect us both if we got thrown in the middle of any altercations. "When was your last vacation together?" I asked.

"About a year ago," she murmured, with a wistful smile. "We spent a week seaside, reading, relaxing, both of them helping plan my next career steps."

"Think about that time with them now. Remember the peace you felt then. But, Tess, we've got to move. Got to get you out of here or hide, before you're taken inside." I drew Tess to a standing position, my gaze darting left and right, searching for an opening…an opportunity to make a run for it.

"I will, and thank you, Wyatt, for trying to help."

Fresh blood bubbled from both ears now. As I guided her along, Tess stumbled repeatedly, unsteady on her feet. "We're getting out tonight. See up ahead by the main gate?

I'm going to cause a disruption the next time the gates open. When that happens, you get out. I won't be far behind. Got it?"

"All right. I'll try. I promise."

As if on cue, a low hum sounded, a noise I'd already associated with the opening and shutting of the gates. "Yes!" I blurted out, evaluating my options, assessing the strengths of the men and weaponry they carried as they ambled by. My only advantage would be the element of surprise, but if I caught a break, maybe I could slip out with Tess.

The guards didn't appear to be engaged with anything except goading the masses along. Not even the ongoing skirmishes grabbed their attention. I set my sights on the guy at the end of the line because he might buy me more time if I could knock him out without alerting the others ahead of his position. Time for my high school wrestling days to pay off.

I laughed at the lunacy of it all. Leaning toward Tess, I whispered one more warning before getting her positioned to move. But when her gaze lifted to mine, I could tell something was horribly wrong. She lunged forwards, her eyes rounded with her soft intake of breath. That was it, before she went limp in my arms. Tess slid to the ground in conjunction with the gates grinding shut several yards ahead of us. Her gaze froze, locked in a blank stare skyward.

I slapped her hard anyway. "Tess, stay with me!" Bending down, I listened for any sound of breathing, but her chest didn't rise again. I closed her eyes and fell against the fence, stunned.

What now? Most likely Tess's parents had died, trying to assure that their daughter would live, that Tess would make it through this ordeal—like my dad's sacrifice for us.

"Happens that way sometimes, kid," a man's gruff voice spouted out. He squatted and rested two fingers on her neck, checking for a pulse. "She's gone."

I nodded, fighting the urge to slug the man for intruding. "Who are you?"

"Name's Mason." He stepped back, yanking a cotton sheet from his pack. When he thrust it loose, I helped him arrange it over the body.

"I should tell somebody. Shouldn't I?" My throat tightened as I glanced at her shrouded form. "I can't just leave her here like this."

"Might want to think that through. You two were friends?"

I scoffed. "Sure, I guess, but I haven't known her long."

"These fine, upstanding citizens in control here might slap you with a murder charge."

I felt my hackles rise. "What?"

"An easy way to explain a death. Right? Seems cruel at first, but you should move along. Put some distance between you two. That young thing's gone now." His eyebrows lifted. "I guess you did all you could for her."

I exhaled a long breath and straightened. "Yeah, well, it wasn't good enough. Was it?"

Mason's gaze shifted, connecting with mine, when he caught me focusing on the Lost, making steady progress through the checkpoint on the other side of the yard. The unruly pockets of people had dispersed, for the most part, leaving only a couple of stray fights still underway in the thinning clusters.

He jerked his chin toward the queue. "You worried about going through that line?"

My jaw tensed. Hell yeah, I wanted to scream. This might be it for me now too. After everything…to just end it here… I opened my mouth, but the words died on my lips.

"*Humph*," Mason grunted. "You look like someone I know. Are you Scott's boy, by any chance? What's your name, son?"

I turned my head, meeting Mason eye to eye. "Yeah. Wyatt. Why? What do you know of my dad?"

"Kid, whether you believe it or not, luck is shining on us tonight. Providence intervening, fate is guiding our hand, or Scott himself is managing the playing field down here through some divine discourse. This is the break we needed."

12

Ellie

The food warmed me on its way down, calming the chill that had permeated my bones. After the past week, why anything still had the power to shock or surprise me, I don't know. But alien beings summoned to Earth to feed off our memories? No words existed to describe the horror that filled me as I clung to the page, transfixed, rereading Scott's explanation for a third time.

The Unfound is what we call ourselves. Situated

between the Lost and the Found, the term defines those of us committed to stopping this atrocity before it ends life on this planet as we know it. Breaking it down into three sects, we have a pool of people already Lost—those evidenced on the Jumbotrons—then those destined by their status in the Inner Circle to be among the Found, and finally those left, fighting their planned ultimate outcome, the Unfound.

The members of the Inner Circle are promised the reward of eternal life by an alien entity—a payoff the group will do anything to realise. Everything and everyone in their way are expendable. It's evident now, in the midst of exposing their work, that for decades, the Inner Circle has guided us toward this path. Their careful tutelage and betrayal of the public took years to bring to fruition. I only wish my team had uncovered it sooner. So that more would have had a chance at life.

Over the past week, my associates have reached out, saving who they could. Now that the culling phase has begun, it's a waiting game. The doc you'll meet, and a handful of others like him, are committed to preserving all lives possible, judging sincerity of claims where necessary to conceal our hand a little longer, so we can avoid annihilation, while the possibility of success, even if small, still exists.

This is a long shot at best, as I'm sure you're ascertaining about now. Someone messed up, clueing in the Inner Circle, and so I believe they stepped up their timeline of events as a result. With me at the forefront of who they want gone first. Some among my team have already succumbed; some are among the walking dead, outwitted at the last, like myself. But what matters is those still in place and that they are pledged to see this through, fighting 'til the bitter end, no matter what.

We're diligently exploring, working all possibilities, in our effort to thwart the Inner Circle's takeover, our newest hope only just coming to life involving the elderly among us, who society had given up on. It's ironic that the oldest in our midst may be our saviours, when we're the ones who abandoned them.

But we're far from a resolution. The Inner Circle possesses skills more developed than our own. Telepathic ones, to be exact; furthermore, their heritage comes from a line that isn't fully human. Not knowing exactly what we're up against will be an ongoing battle—one we'll need to prepare for and continually reassess. Perhaps options exist in turning some of those members to our side, pleading our human plight. All avenues need to be explored...

The details that followed involved the gathering of the elderly resources, but not specifically how they were to be used. Last, I read the letter Scott had written for me. I don't know that I'd ever be strong enough, but healed from the removal of my IC device, with a newly infused hope from Scott's journey, I slipped the paper from the envelope and read through my watery eyes.

As I revisited our life together through Scott's perspective, during what he knew to be his final hours with us, I began to see our lives on a continuum, like I believe he did. We were born, lived, found each other, and loved a lifetime's worth—this lifetime. Our love wasn't bound by the death of our bodies, the way he described our bond. Nothing would separate us for good. Now I understood that too.

Tears streaking down my cheeks, the last pages of information still lapping against my mind, I read his final lines out loud. "I'll see you when your work is through, sweetheart. Yours in life, death, and all the realms before, after and in between. Scott."

Charlie poked his head in the room. "Oh, sorry. I can come back later."

I swiped at my eyes. "No. Come on in. Now is fine."

Charlie eyed my empty bowl. "Good. You finished that broth quick."

"Yeah. I needed it more than I thought I did."

"Doc knows best," he teased, reaching for a seat.

"So, you are part of Scott's team?"

"Newly adopted. Yes. A handful of us are attempting a surgical solution before the memory extraction, as you've experienced firsthand."

"Thank you, Doctor. Every procedure you perform is a life saved."

He shrugged. “Potentially. It’s only the first step, though.”

“I understand that now. We have to stem the appetite of the thing coming to Earth for our memories.”

Doc gave me a slow nod. “Well put.”

“How are those old people involved in that process? I didn’t find much in Scott’s notes on that.”

“Correct. That information developed rapidly right about the time—”

“Scott took his life,” I finished for the doc.

“Yes. Your husband was one of the bravest men I’ve ever known.”

“I wholeheartedly agree.”

“Regarding your question, I expect to be contacted soon. Most likely from among my counterparts, since I assume surgical skill is necessary.”

“Makes sense, I guess. But what could the elderly offer that would bring about a solution? Many are near death, and all are comatose. Right?”

“True. And a large portion are ailing from one disease or another.”

“I don’t see it.”

“Within their infirmity lies an answer, I believe. I have my own theories, now that I’ve been directed down this particular path.”

“Do you know how to connect with other members of Scott’s team?”

He shook his head. "Only the other doctors. Anonymity is essential in recruiting others to take part. This way, if someone is found out, we aren't all exposed, and our work can continue forward."

"I hope those in support of Scott and his efforts are enough to turn the tide. 'Cause, right now, the outlook is pretty damn bleak."

"More than either of us knows. I'm certain of that much." Charlie's eyes held a determined glint. "What resources do you need to go after your son?"

13

Wyatt

"Not too long ago, I was part of the Inner Circle," Mason explained.

"Then you're no friend of mine or my father's," I spat back, narrowing my eyes at him through a glare.

"Not so fast. I said *was*. I'm not any longer."

"Why should I trust you?"

"Well, I'm here for one thing. Locked up, same as you."

"That doesn't mean shit. Spies are everywhere."

"True, and your instincts are on point. But I'm batting for the other side now."

I scrutinised him. "Go on."

"I'm guessing you know what's coming for the stash of collected memories."

Jogging my head, I played along. I understood from my dad's journal that the recipient was otherworldly. But how all this happened… Maybe, if I kept quiet, he'd give me more info.

"Kid, I don't have anything to lose. Once the Inner Circle uncovered ties, linking me to your father, they cast me out, then condemned me here. I'm not that special. Once my apparatus activates, I'll be just another empty shell, like everyone else here." He gave me a crooked smile. "They didn't count on me meeting you here, though. You see, without my counterparts, my powers are limited."

"Powers?"

"Powers," Mason repeated. "If you're not ready to hear what I have to say, I understand. But if you're truly Scott's kid, offspring of the man who had me reconsidering my alliances forged decades ago, then you'll jump at this chance to aid the crumbling remnant of humanity."

I took the man's measure, wondering along with him if I had the courage, the fortitude, to face what he was about to say, equally torn between the desire to know more and to duck my head in the dirt. But that wouldn't make this horror go away. Dad had mentioned in his journal that those among the Inner Circle possessed abilities beyond our own. "I'm listening."

"I'm not fully human."

I nodded, his words verifying dad's. For the Inner Circle to summon a being from space, made sense that those doing the calling were at least part extraterrestrial too. "Me and those like me can communicate telepathically with each other. This ability isn't as useful between Inner Circle members and humans, however. Your ability as a race to concentrate and send thoughts is immature at best, even when aided with someone like me, although I'd been practicing this skill with your father. That's how I got found out."

Hmm. Telepathy. "Why would you decide to help us, the *inferior* race?"

He gave me a glance, like he could see right through me. "Maybe it was your tenacity. In spite of your frail human makeup, some of you are worthy of effort. Letting all of you die off would be...unfortunate."

"I see. You pity us."

"I guess that's true. In a way, I also envy you." The man jerked his head to the side before peering into the night sky, a melancholy tone to his voice. "The thing is, the entity wouldn't settle for just any memories. Only human ones would do. Your innocence, the joy you exude in your short span of life, it's nectar for the one who has promised its followers eternal life in exchange for the culmination of emotions you all possess."

"If that's so, why don't you want it? To live forever?"

"Because ironically I'd rather have what you have instead. A life steeped with emotion in one gigantic burst. Knowing there's an end makes the journey more poignant, more powerful, the moments of time more real and intense." He shrugged. "I've always been more of a shooting-star kinda guy myself."

"So, the Inner Circle gave you your wish."

"I didn't voice it, but they saw through my duplicity eventually: my desire to aid humankind. My punishment is amusingly suitable, wouldn't you say? I can feel my internal clock ticking away, never certain which minute will be my last. That sums up your every day."

"Your dream we're discussing here. Not mine."

"Before I explode forth a mass full of memories, we need to accomplish a few specifics."

"Okay... What exactly?" I cocked my head, listening as I tried to second guess him, wondering if I was making the right move. But in my current predicament, what did I have to lose?

"Getting you past the Collectors for one, then preparing to give you humans a fighting chance. I can help with both."

While we'd talked, the yard had emptied, the line ahead dwindling, as guards funnelled the remaining Lost toward their security gates, where, from the looks of it, an initial processing was well underway. "Really? What's your plan? Once they scan me, and the Collectors realise I don't have my device, I'm done for."

"I can project your data to them. Through a form of telepathy. The guards will never know the difference."

"Interesting…"

"Yes, a bit of a crude transmission platform, utilising humans as an interface, but I'm betting it'll still work. Transmitting a static image or a set of limited data isn't as draining as connecting and communicating thoughts."

"But where will you transfer—"

"Trust me. I've got this."

Trust? I hardly knew the man. I sucked in air, working to stay calm. This was a lot to take in, but evaluating my options, which currently tallied to zero, I fell in line and waited for my fate, adopting the glazed-over deadened-eyes facade that everyone else had here. Anxious, I held my breath, but the Collectors didn't even give me a passing glance, while we worked our way through the verification points.

The scan proceeded as if I'd had a functioning device in my head, my personal data added to a digital file right before my eyes. "Nice work," I breathed out, once we'd cleared the station.

"Come on," Mason encouraged, taking the lead, guiding us through an isolated corridor to an abandoned corner of space.

Outside, conditions had been disgusting. Inside, a whole other level of deplorable existed. I guess the close quarters did it. Was it possible to die from ingesting the foulness of others? I could barely suck in a breath without gagging.

"Second item."

"Right. Our one chance. Lay it on me."

"We're going to poison the memories, hopefully enough to send the entity off in search of tastier morsels."

"All right. I'll bite. How?"

"One of my assigned tasks was to get the underground medical teams a key piece of intel. Then I ended up here."

I opened my mouth to speak.

"Don't concern yourself with how I know this. It's not important. That we transmit my information to the doctor who fixed you up, before my final song, that's what matters. Comatose dementia patients are already assembled. Scott had got that first set of instructions disseminated to the surgical teams, before his, uh, departure. Now all that remains is to implant the IC devices and wait. That is what the doctors need to know. At the time, Scott wasn't aware of this last piece."

"They don't have them in place?"

"No. That's a necessary prerequisite. Remember, these pieces of tech monitor our health, alert us to any slight change that could indicate a problem. Due to scientific and technologic advances, most diseases this day and age have been cured or corrected—that process helped along by advanced detection from our devices."

"Right."

"However, this subset of the population was lost to memory-comprising diseases long ago and never reaped that benefit, or curse, depending how you view the situation, from constant monitoring and evaluation of their medical status. Those I speak of are very specific—already too ill to have the apparatus installed, back when they became mandatory. Once in place, the automatic functioning will take over and send their fragmented memories to be transmitted. No waiting."

"Sounds cruel, for the frailest of us, even among today's standards."

"Maybe. But this particular set of humans could be who sets you free. In addition, these memory-comprised patients had previously consented to give their bodies to research, when the time came, and have been carefully weeded out from other ill geriatric subjects. To be clear, the families involved have already assented to whatever good could become of the tragic illnesses their loved ones endured."

"If all this proceeds as you've laid out, when those memories are uploaded, they won't be what this being expects? Correct?"

"Well, it's worse than that. The infusion of this mess of memories will infect the 'good' ones already compiled, basically infecting the whole lot."

"Spoiling the meat, it sounds like."

A grin split his face. "Exactly."

"Okay, well, telepathy the shit out of someone and get this information moving."

"Not that simple. My telepathic interface with humans is awkward at best, which is why I haven't been able to get the message across. Until now."

My gush of breath came out as a growl. "Then I don't understand how this knowledge can help us, if we can't relay it. Wait… What?"

"That's right. You're gonna get this information to your mother, who will tell the doc, and he'll use his network to inform the team of doctors."

"Me?"

"Correct. The chances of the connection working increase if there's a personal, and even better, a genetic connection, like you with your mother. When joining in telepathy, thoughts seek like matter, recognise homologous telepathic signatures. Yours would be similar to your mother's and father's. Understand?"

"Not really. But I'm not sure any amount of explaining will help. I figure things out the old-fashioned way, by doing."

"Sounds good. If you're up for it, let's get started."

"Okay." My mood shifted, mirroring the weather change that had blown in the rain, suddenly pouring down, battering the windows in heavy sheets. I gazed outside as an ominous foreboding seized me. Claps of thunder joined in, while jolts of lightning paraded across the sky. I yanked my attention back to Mason, fear gnawing away my insides.

Maybe this would be how I'd die, some willing pawn in this man's game. Who really knew which side he played for? What's more, I knew nothing about telepathy. He could just as well be offering me up to the giant monster as a predinner snack, and I'd never know the difference.

Mason spoke, but the rumble of the storm swallowed his words. Assembling the jumble of my emotions, I stilled, homing in, trying to focus on the task. Before me, Mason's eyes held a calming light. I reached for it, willing the feeling to infuse me too. "I'm ready," I announced, sweat breaking out on my forehead.

"Good. Begin with thoughts of your mother. We need the essence of her, so search for a bond, a potent memory that connects you two. Whatever it is, concentrate on it now. I'm only a conduit. Prepare your thoughts for the message you want to send. When you're ready, nod."

I watched as a tremor of power washed through him. Unsure of what the next minutes would hold, my eyes rounded in awe, I gave a slight jerk of my head and was thrust forward.

Another level of awareness hit me, where I existed on a plane woven between us through the one who knit us together—my father. Mom whispered my name. How she recognised me, I'm not sure. But as my mind brushed hers, her thoughts repeated the communication I'd directed toward her. She understood. I was almost positive. Incredible… Triumph skated over me. The work could begin.

The edges of my mouth inched up as I smiled into Mason's worried gaze. "We did it," I mumbled, energy still draining from the core of me.

"Yes. I think we did."

Despite my fetid surroundings, thoroughly exhausted, I collapsed and plunged into sleep.

14

Ellie

How was this possible? Had that really been my son or a figment of my imagination, a first step into madness caused by my recent surgery? My heart raced, my breathing shallow, uneven, as I stood, clinging to the back of a chair to steady myself.

My door burst open. "What's going—"

The doc stopped short, his forehead folding into straight lines. "Does your head hurt?" he asked, easing me off my feet before checking my pulse. "Tell me if you can."

"No. Not like you mean."

"I heard something fall in here."

I glanced at the other chair in the room, fallen on its side. "Yeah, I guess that was me. It was so sudden, shocking… I'm not sure I believe what just happened, and I lived it."

Unease swirled in the man's eyes. "What happened?"

"It's my son. He spoke to me."

Doc turned his head left, then right, searching. "Where'd he go?"

"Uh…he was never here."

"I'm not sure I'm with you, Ellie."

Running a hand through my hair, I gave him a weak smile. "Yeah… I'm not sure I'm with me either."

Doc righted the chair, straddled it, and poured on the bedside manner. "You're concerned about your son. That's a given and understandable. So, let's start at the top."

I averted my eyes. "My son talked to me. Through my thoughts. There… I said it."

"Okay…" he drawled. "Say anything useful?"

I lifted my gaze to his. "You're running with me on this?"

"I am."

"The odd thing is what he had to say concerned those almost-dead old patients of yours. Weird, right?"

"What?"

"I know. Crazy. I'll shut up."

"No… Makes a helluva lot more sense now." Doc

scooted his chair forward a little more, the excitement in his voice sending a chill over my skin. "This is what I've been waiting for. A sign… A direction of some sort. Tell me exactly what he said."

"Here's the bottom line. All those elderly patients need to be fitted with IC devices, pronto. Then, assuming they survive the procedure, their jumbled memories will be sucked away, combined with the rest."

"Of course." The doc scooted back, his eyes igniting from somewhere within. "Kinda like burning the biscuits, I guess. Not quite as tasteful when mixed all together."

"If you say so. You're the doc here."

"A stroke of genius. I've been wondering who might guide us on our next steps. But your son? I wouldn't have guessed. I didn't think Scott—"

"This didn't come from Scott," I clarified, "and wasn't directed by my son either. Someone else fed him this information and linked our thoughts together, all so you could be informed, Doc."

His eyes went wide, as if the new details were just registering. "I'd better get busy. Best case, this will take days. I'll set up the 3D printer to produce all those devices. Plus, I need to get the word out, pass this knowledge along to the other doctors on the team. This is great news, Ellie." He grabbed my shoulders and squeezed as a broad smile swept his face. "Really it is."

Doc shoved away his chair and strode for the door,

then slowed and swivelled back to face me, his concern evident. "Why don't you take a breather, just sit there for a while?"

"Hell no," I muttered, rising. "I want to help. I'm no doctor, but surely you can put me to work doing something useful that will up the chances of those ancient ones making it through surgery."

A slow smile lifted his cheeks. "I sure can. If you mean that, follow me."

For the first time since this whole nightmare began, it felt good to finally be participating in an activity that might help in the battle we were facing. Not just reacting to each pile of shit shovelled my way. "Doc?"

"Yeah," he asked over his shoulder.

"I know where my son is."

He slowed while I caught up. "Great news," he said, his eyes crinkling with worry. "Go get him. I can get started without you, you know."

I spit out a laugh. "Of course I do. But from what I could gather, which wasn't much, it won't be easy."

"What do you know of his whereabouts?"

"That he's being held with the Lost in a camp close by. He let himself get taken, searching for Tess." I watched his facial features tense.

"And how is she?"

"Not good, from what he communicated. You need to understand this wasn't like a normal conversation. He struggled to get his message across, like the act alone took a significant amount of energy. Broken words, I mean, thoughts, was how it funnelled through to me."

"We can drum up some help for you."

"Someone is aiding him on the inside, an Inner Circle member."

Doc's eyebrows shot up. "That doesn't sound right. They've been the ones orchestrating the destruction from the beginning."

"Seems as if this one has had a change of heart. The man extended his own telepathic skill to my son somehow, so he could reach me, ensuring that we had a chance to implement the next stage of the plan."

"I sure as hell hope you're right." A muscle twitched along his jaw. "This feels like the right move, though, and my gut tells me it could work. If an Inner Circle member is actually assisting our cause, all the better. Maybe Wyatt can pull more info from the guy." Doc's face bent into a frown. "Huh... Does that mojo you have with your son work in reverse? Could you initiate it?"

"No, I don't think so. The power I felt when we connected is gone, for now anyway."

"Okay. I'll proceed. You continue on, however you feel led. Either way, I understand."

Over the next three days I experienced more exhaustion than I ever thought possible, but it revived me in a way also, as I dug in and committed to this fight that my husband had been so embroiled within—although trying to show up the cyborgs in the care of the elderly patients didn't put me in my best light. In fact, I probably hampered their efficiency a time or two, but due to our collective efforts, all except three of the thirty or so patients made it through the procedure. Good thing putting those devices in didn't take near as long as cutting them out. Some might still die. Cruel as it sounded, we only needed to get them past the point of activation.

A few days in, I didn't notice the smells, the fluids not fazing me any longer either. I just sat with the patients, holding their hands, while their memories slid from them, their awareness long gone. No cyborg could understand the impact of such a loss like a real flesh-and-bone person, but I mourned for what they couldn't comprehend. I hadn't expected the process to be so emotional for people I didn't know, for people who would never be sentient again, even though for a brief time after surgery, a few of the patients woke from their comatose states.

Clinically, they'd become Lost. But their eyes had widened as their fate came to fruition, their faces strained in a combination of fear and surprise before their bodies went slack, and the sudden spark of recognition faded from their eyes. Warriors, through and through, every one of them. "This isn't what I expected."

The doctor's face softened. "Death takes many forms, but it comes for all of us, eventually. Passing from this life into the next should impact those of us who remain. Beds full of people just like these may be what save us all from endless oblivion, consumed by some hungry, emotionless beast."

I laid down the hand I'd been holding, the woman's blank stare eerily aimless, but her breathing easier now. "Since you've completed all the procedures, I'm leaving tomorrow to find my son. If nothing else, I'll be with him for whatever comes next."

"Thank you for your help. I'm not expecting these patients to live more than another twenty-four hours or so. But they've given their all. And so have you. We'll rustle up some people to accompany you. Whatever you need. Wyatt's been crucial in furthering our efforts. We'll do all we can for him."

Later that night, footfalls pounded the corridor, waking me from a deep sleep. Shrill screams came next. As shots stuttered outside my door, I jumped out of bed and jerked on clothes. God, this is it…

I dived for my bag, rummaging through the clutter until my hand wrapped around the 9 millimetre, then extra clips. Busy stowing away both, I startled when my door swung open.

"Charlie…" I gasped out a breath. "It's only you."

"You headed aboveground?"

My gaze drifted to the gun he carried, such an odd juxtaposition to the medical scrubs he wore. "I need to," I said, refocusing my thoughts. "My son's mixed up in all this. I feel it. I've got to be there with him."

"Those people I promised—"

"I know… We're all taking things as they come."

"Come back safe and bring your boy with you."

"I'm not returning without him. You take care of those patients of ours."

Doc canted his head and slipped back into the fray. Strapping my smaller bag across my chest, already filled with basic medical supplies and water, I followed close on his heels.

Isolated gunfire rang out, which didn't make sense to me. Why would we be fighting against our own? Through two more sets of doors and tossed into the Nest, the rising panic became clear. Fights and skirmishes had broken out everywhere as the locals here wrestled for scraps of stuff.

I plodded a path through, ducking when I could to avoid a stray hit, planting my boots and punching back when I didn't have another option. Working my way clear at last, I climbed the ladder that would bring me to street level. With a hard shove of my hip, the door opened, and I got my first look at city streets I barely recognised.

15

Wyatt

Days passed. Each one feeling just like the last. I craved the night, at least then I didn't have to roam among the walking dead. Wandering around the pen, I pitied them, was haunted by the windows of their eyes, peering into our darkest future—our brains not yet clued in on the fact that our insides were lifeless—only mimicking what we once had.

I'd not allowed myself to go there—tried anyway—but here, so close among them, it'd been impossible to avoid. My father's actions… I understood them now. He hadn't chosen to leave us, not really. He'd decided not to let his consciousness blend into the nothingness, fighting until he couldn't any longer, then dying with his humanity intact. I can see that with a new awareness, face-to-face with living the alternative, day in and day out.

Mason mumbled something unintelligible beside me, where we sat against the building, absorbing the heat stored in the bricks from the day just past. On the nights when the weather allowed it, I slept out here. In the nighttime air, I could draw in breath not so mired in stink and could gaze at the stars, their cold steady calm my only peace in this place, while we waited for the next hand to play out in this sick cosmic game.

Mason babbled on; the man talked incessantly, although he'd not shared more about the Inner Circle, and we'd not attempted telepathy another time, so sure that our first try had hit the mark. I had been convinced too, initially. After all, I'd experienced my mother's thoughts, alive within mine. Among the dredges from that activity since that night, my inner workings up there throbbed. As if my brain waves ached, hungered for more, anxiously waiting until the need would be satisfied again.

Was it normal? Afraid to ask Mason, I kept silent, believing it'd go away. Kind of like a nagging bruise, I reasoned. But it hadn't yet. What could it mean?

Mason's chatter stopped, while the gruel that masqueraded for food passed our way. "You can have mine," I offered, sliding the bowl out of my sight. "I'm not hungry."

"You need to keep your strength up. Tonight might be when our efforts bear fruit." The tone of his voice altered, apprehensive…chilling.

"How do you mean?"

His gaze tossed to the sky. "See for yourself."

Getting my boots underneath me, I scrambled to a stand. "You're right," I agreed, casting my eyes upward. "That doesn't look…natural." The clouds shifted in the night sky, colliding and reforming, until their mass obscured the individual stars' pinpoints of light. "Those aren't clouds up there. Are they?"

He smacked his lips together. "No. No, they're not."

The mass slithered closer, and as it began a slow descent from its position high in the sky, the centre of the thing pulsed. The nearer it got, the louder the beat echoed, at last drowning out the monotonous drone of memories spewing on autopilot in the background from nearby Jumbotrons.

The Collectors looked to the heavens as well, transfixed by the strange mass. Apparently, they weren't in the know either, same as us, only pawns in the grand master plan. Those among the Lost, whose hand had already been dealt, continued their slow meander, oblivious to the horror shaping the course of history through them.

"Can you communicate with it? I mean, you were part

of the Inner Circle, instrumental in getting the thing here."

"*Were* being the operative word there, kid. I'm right here, right now, living the moment with all of you. No more privy to what's happening than any other human, except the foreknowledge of its arrival."

My heart rate ticked up, and I broke out in a sweat. "When will we know if what we've done made any difference?"

"I don't think we'll have to wait long. The being is on an intercept course, but slowly so we can see it coming for us."

To me, it felt different. Slow going, yes. But that beast's heart rate, if the thing actually had a heart, had picked up too, pounding obscenely fast. Was it enjoying its leisurely parade, finally able to anticipate the feast it'd been promised? Maybe it savoured this moment, so close to victory. Whatever the next span of time held for us, life, or some lingering form of death, I found myself captivated, while the entity closed in, hovering above, blanketing the Earth with its powerful quivering life force.

A clamouring around us brought my attention to the camp. The Collectors who remained beat a collective path toward the gates and freedom. Where exactly were they running to? I laughed, the sound incongruous to what was happening here. But I couldn't help it as Mason and I watched their stampede.

The Collectors breeched the gate, a commingled knot

of men, weapons brandished, protecting their own exodus. Within their number, shots rang out, individual brawls escalating as they fought for the privilege of being the first outside. Men dropped in a frenzied flurry of death, blood oozing from the wounded and dead, slicking the ground among the fighting madness. Their faces taut, lips peeled back, reflecting their own hysteria, they killed who they could and pounded others into submission, instead of the being bearing down upon them, suspended in the sky.

Above, the thing emitted a leisurely groaning moan, seizing the Collectors' attention, as they abruptly came to their senses, glanced at their remaining number, then holstered their weapons, looks of horror skittering across their faces. Unaffected by the confrontation between the ranks, the Lost followed the surviving men, herded along like sheep. Mason and I brought up the rear, the lot of us spilling into the streets, the air so ripe with anticipation we could practically taste it.

Rancid smells of accumulated filth, fresh blood, and rotten food slammed together in a sickening mix that had me light-headed. Flesh pressed against flesh, we waited for our future to play out, unable to pull ourselves from the unfolding scene.

"Stupid shits," Mason scoffed. "Missing the mark, all of them." He scrutinised the growing crowd, the appreciation plain by his smirk. "Would you look here… Like the last call for dinner on a warm summer's night, isn't it? That point where hunger finally outweighed your desire for one more adventure, and you could smell the food leading you home. Memories are that way for—"

My focus shifted from tracking the looming mass to where the voice had suddenly squelched out beside me. "Mason?" His gaze fixed on mine, cognisant, not empty, like the memory-deficient Lost surrounding us.

Sagging in my arms as I reached for him, he mumbled, "Found me, I guess. This is my moment, kid. You be sure and hang on for the ride. This place is gonna need men like you on the other side."

"Mason! No, not yet. I have no idea what to do. Don't you leave me. Don't!"

"It's brilliant," he managed, his eyes trained on some version of now that I couldn't see. "Just as I imagined." With a triumphant smile plastered on his face, Mason thudded to the ground.

Son of a bitch… I crouched, feeling for a pulse. Damn it! He wasn't walking with the Lost but dead. What the hell do I do now? I lifted my gaze upward again, the entity so close almost intimately entwined with us. Small pockets of its essence created a mist, dipping tantalisingly among the gathered. I was certain, if I reached out, I could brush its surface with a touch. I stretched… Almost there…

But the moment passed, the dark massive blob sweeping in the air, preparing for its next move, the action unsettling anything not attached, sending items levitating into the breeze. I scuttled my way free of the crowd. I couldn't miss it, this history in the making.

The sky crackled, alive with energy, as an opening cut through the being—a mouth, maybe? Seconds later, streams of matter rose from the ground to meet it, culminating in the air. Captivated, I froze, joining in the deafening silence descending over the space. The memory playback, constant during this entire nightmare, quieted. A sucking, gulping sound filled the void—as the monster got down to business, stuffing its face.

16

Ellie

Manoeuvring through the hordes of people, my pistol drawn, gaze pasted to the sky, I made slow forward progress. Obscene noises came from the thing, like it was thoroughly enjoying what it ingested and couldn't contain expressing its pleasure. I wondered as I watched it eat, if what we did had any impact at all—the surgeries, the memories lifted up to poison this monster's meal. Maybe we'd been too late after all. If so, what mattered was Wyatt. Getting to him before the next course in this alien feast.

I pictured a world under the rule of this entity. Hiding underground along an old subway line wouldn't be deep enough or far enough away from this thing to keep it from finding us. Without our IC devices to funnel the memories through and transform those morsels into a form it could eat, what then? I guess the apparatuses would be forced back into us, or perhaps the thing would just settle for swallowing people whole.

But then what? A world full of listless zombies once it had gorged on everyone? At that point, death would be a blessing. Made sense. The beast was an animal, after all. Once it had gained what it could, had ravaged the planet in totality, it'd move on, seeking other tasty treats. Scott saw this coming. God rest his soul. Knowing everything I know now, I fear most that he got every bit of this right.

Restless with this mass murderer, my gaze combed the horde, enthralled by the feeding underway. Wait, was that Wyatt? I shoved harder, angling for a better view, but crammed within the crowd, I couldn't budge. My eyes narrowed… Yes! Hoisted onto the top of a hover car, Wyatt looked primed to take off, one knee bent, resting on the roof, the other foot planted firmly, ready to race away when necessary. "Wyatt!"

My voice fell, dissipating in the midst of the rumbling echoes of the entity's consumption. I raised my weapon in the air and shot off a round. Wyatt swivelled toward the disruption, our eyes meeting for a second, before the Lost were spooked and worked to trample the object of their mutual fear—me. I didn't want to shoot them. But they weren't giving me any other option. Except for the fact the sheer volume of the vacated individuals had me pinned.

I screamed again, hoping I might stun them all enough to free my hands. Slowly the circle of the Lost thinned, cast aside one by one, as Wyatt ripped a path to me.

"Mom?" He yanked me to my feet.

"Wyatt, I'm so glad you're okay."

He darted a glance to the sky and smirked, circling me in a hug. "Relatively speaking, I guess so. You know how to use that thing."

His voice held a hint of surprise. I tucked the 9 millimetre back into my waistband. "Yes. And I'm a damn good shot too."

His answering grin cut through the tension. "Come on. The view's better from over there."

"But do we really want to hang around for the whole show? When it's done licking its fingers, what then?"

He drew me alongside him, cutting his way back to his perch. "You don't understand, Mom. I *need* to see this."

"Need to? Whatever happens next can sure as hell proceed without us front and centre. Do you want to be here for the stampede that's coming up on the agenda? 'Cause I don't think that beast up there is gonna fill up anytime soon."

"I get it. You needed to find me, and you have. Go

back underground if you want. I'll be along…later," he added, with a defiant tilt of his head. "I'm not missing the defining event of our lifetimes."

"You pig-headed, stupid kid!"

"Mom!"

"I'm just getting started—"

"Mom! Look!"

My rant cut short, I followed the trajectory of my son's gaze. The outline of the mass in the sky shivered as it paused, eating; the streams flowing upward frozen by some silent warp in time. "What's happening?" I asked. My breath stilled, and the crowd's collectively with it. We waited, our fates hanging in the balance, the silence pervasive, hinging on the entity's next move.

Seconds felt like hours in the space of the time that passed, all our faces uplifted to the heavens. What sounded like raspy moans exhaled from the creature, and as the minutes ticked by, it got louder, angrier.

The murky mass shifted, its substance convulsing violently.

"Mom, is it doing what I think it is?" Wyatt fought a rising smile, eventually losing the battle as his lips lifted.

"The motions look familiar, just on a much larger scale than when you or I get sick."

A roar barrelled from it, and the substance hanging in the air changed direction, moving in reverse this time. I winced and covered my ears against the deafening cacophony. On the ground, others did the same, prostrating themselves, overwhelmed with the prospect of what might come next.

I wrapped my arms around Wyatt's waist, determined not to let go, no matter what this beast offered up. Then a burst rang out, like a thousand tiny voices, and I twisted, still clinging to Wyatt, searching for its source.

The huge Jumbotrons—I could spot from my perch that two of the eyesores had shattered, sending forth shards of glass, like miniature armed missiles. They soared through the disturbed air, stirred up by the force of the monster's sickness, piercing through the gathered at random, burying into the flesh of those unlucky enough to be in its path.

Wyatt tackled me, and we stayed that way, stuck to the roof of the car, until the tingling in the air quieted. He rolled off me, and I peeled myself from the metal, both lifting our gazes again.

The flow had stopped, the mass still shuddering but inching upward into the sky. By virtue of its vast size, the creature had blotted out the sun, and little by little, as it crept away, the first streaks of sunrise burst through the shadows, its light exposing the horror left behind.

I tracked the thing as it lifted higher and higher, not trusting it wouldn't swoop back down for seconds and devour those of us still standing, like some tasty after-dinner sweets. Watching it growing smaller and smaller, I knew, deep in my gut, I'd never trust its absence. That monster, or another like it, could come here at any time. How would we ever be ready? It had almost decimated us.

History had proven humans had a short recall. How long before those of us with memory faculties still intact would listen while someone touts a new and improved IC device—one that couldn't be corrupted, and then we all jump on board again, sending humanity right back here?

We aren't alone in the universe. This awakening had taught the people that, at least. We shouldn't pretend otherwise.

"Mom?"

Wyatt shook me, forcing me to peer into his eager eyes, lit up with a barely contained thrill from the event we'd just experienced. What was I to do with him? My fears amped up a notch.

"Are you okay?" he asked.

I bobbed my head, shading my eyes from the dappled bits of sun poking through the clouds. "I will be. Let's help who we can. I doubt emergency services will get through." I opened my bag and pulled out the meagre first aid supplies I brought.

Worry etched the lines of Wyatt's face, my son looking like himself again. "You first," he insisted, taking the kit from me.

During the hours that came next, I watched him work, with not a doubt in my mind something significant had changed inside him. For sure, this experience had made an impact. On all of us. But upon closer inspection, what I saw was a quality more defining…insidious even…as a new terror snaked up my spine.

"Come on. We need rest." I grabbed his arm, half expecting him to put up a fight.

"Right behind you." He blew out a long breath. "I don't think I've ever been this exhausted."

"You did well. Your father would be proud." As I tousled his hair, he gave me a goofy smile, reminding me of more carefree times at home, lightening the moment. "I want to hear about it. Everything that happened."

His brows knotted, stabs of pain contorting his face. "I'll try."

Wyatt

It had me…what I'd fought so hard against. The huge blob slurped me inside; I existed as an ancient being, my consciousness only a subset of many. I feel it now—where the creature stores the memories it consumed. All are intertwined. I can access my beginning and can see I have no end in my place along the continuum. This must be what Mason meant by eternal life, but this reality is so much more fulfilling. We revel in emotions…love, sorrow, hate, pity, desire, grief, pain, constantly accessing these by ingesting the essence of lives lived by others—their memories. Is it really death if these pieces live on?

I thrashed side to side, caught up in the sheets that trapped me, cinching me tight. Jolting awake, I swiped at a layer of sweat covering my forehead. It had happened again. I gulped in air, kicking free from the covers, and sat shivering on the edge of the bed. I'd visited wherever the hell that was, as…something else. Four times I'd been there now since that day a month ago, when the monster had come and gone from this place.

But it didn't leave me.

What we'd done, tainting the memories, appeared to have worked—for the short term, at least. The entity's feasting activities ceased before it belched out the substance culled from our devices that had just gone in. Who knew if it would stay away, though? Now we lived with the ever-present knowledge that it's out there. Lurking… And if it's out there, what else might be coming for us?

My new awareness haunted me, and I wasn't sure what to do with it. My best guess was Mason's interaction with my mind started it all. Did he somehow initiate this transformation? And if so, what was next? These visions took me further inside the consciousness of the being with each visitation. When I was there, mired within the thing, it became harder and harder to keep a solid grip on reality, to return unscathed to what was left for me here.

After Mom and I recovered, me from dehydration, her from minor injuries sustained during the attack, we packed up our sparse belongings and moved a little further south, almost to the beginning of the old subway line when it had been operational in the DC area. This set of rooms, where Dad had carved out a spot for us, was comfortable enough, and while nothing like home, we had what we needed to get by.

The state of my new living accommodations reflected my altered status in other ways as well. Before, my room…our home, had been an oasis—where I could disappear, with anything I'd ever need available at my fingertips, via my IC device, or by engaging aid from our vast array of virtual and AI resources. We'd all come to depend on these forms of support, blind to the long-term consequences which led us here.

I glimpsed my austere surroundings with a critical eye. A desk, chair, dresser, bed, shelving units, and makeshift closet. Stuff didn't weigh me down any longer, for better or worse. And I did my own research these days, for what it was worth, for the very first time with me at the reins, not subjugated by the algorithms of AI and VR tech, which started us down this path so many decades ago.

Compared to our stark reality today, we'd experienced a life of luxury. Cyborg assistants, AI interwoven seamlessly into our daily lives, integration of our thoughts into the operation of our apparatuses, vacations on an impulse, all awaiting us inside the ease of an engineered simulation.

The simplicity now… It fit my new persona, honed by the defining experiences of our new age, but anchored in the discipline that I discovered my parents had been shaping in me all along.

My mother and I had been among the fortunate Unfound, in that we still lived. But going forward, our futures were precarious and uncertain. Thousands had died over the past month, while millions more had been tallied as Lost in this city alone. And the numbers were still climbing. The destruction and waste aboveground made it impossible to know exact information. Maybe we never would. Priorities had shifted throughout the tattered Perfected States, with our plight played out in other major cities across the nation.

Our system of government deteriorated, and what was left of the old Inner Circle quickly dispersed. Any ties to the extraterrestrial being have been rigorously denied. The small band of us who comprehended the truth of the situation, acknowledged among ourselves that it's only a matter of time before they'd rally and attempt to infiltrate our cities once more.

IC devices were no longer mandatory; however, a minority, whose devices hadn't been activated yet, chose to remain oblivious to all that had just occurred and decided to keep them in place. The rest of those, with a still-intact active apparatus, have lined up for the now popular option of surgical removal.

Aboveground the people had short memory spans, for those who'd retained that faculty, that is. Paths were dug through the ruin in the streets, and a small number of businesses tentatively opened their doors again, a pulse of normalcy returning because others wished it. Not because it was so. We were far from that.

Clean water and food were scarce, med supplies a traded commodity. Survival, once so easy, was a day-to-day struggle. Hardest to witness, the weakest and sickest among us, often the young and very old, were claimed by the streets, their emaciated, rotting bodies on display, adding to the rising death toll. And the horror that lived within remained, despite our reprieve. For those of us with cognition still, we knew we weren't free. To the contrary, our eyes had been opened to the looming uncertain future we now faced.

Among the rubble, a presumed Inner Circle member had been rounded up—destined to become a sacrifice, it seemed. He'd been charged with treason, because somebody needed to pay for the acts committed against the public—lives destroyed, forfeited, for a ruling party's gain. A firing squad was hastily dispatched—a testament to our trials. As I glimpsed the hunger in the wide-eyed faces of the people assembled, saw the open festering wound, it became clearer to me. We had to witness his gruesome death to assign responsibility.

The crowds huddled in tight circles, showing up in force for the spectacle which offered closure to the events that had changed the course of history for mankind. Even I knew it couldn't do that—nothing would. Mom didn't attend. But drawn to the morbid form of justice, I couldn't miss it. So I waited, perched on a pile of rubble, anguish quivering my insides.

Heavy chains bound the man's arms and feet, and as he plodded along the makeshift platform, in a slow, uneven gait, the sound of his shackles clanging mesmerised me. With a shake of his head, he appeared to forgo a blindfold; the prisoner squaring his shoulders and stoically facing the gathered instead. Hissing and screaming, the people responded, incited and eager to get on with the killing.

The doomed man lifted his chin; held his head high, then someone yelled the order, silence tracking the seconds of the space that ticked by. My gaze connected with the stranger, and holding my breath, the air between us sparked alive. *Find me...* I heard, his words drifting through me in an eerie, desperate crawl.

Swallowing the emotion clogging my throat, time shivered while I glimpsed into his soul. A barrage of shots rang out, the man's gaze still pinned to mine, and as if in slow motion, his body crumbled, magnified, in a bloodied heap of flesh and bones. The gunfire echoed, relenting to the sound of roaring voices—the gathered screaming their blood lust, joining in the aftermath.

Shaken by the barbaric kill, I attempted to make sense of the scene. Had that connection really happened? Or had my imagination summoned it all? Lost in my troubled thoughts, I picked my way through the riled-up crowd, unable to loosen the pall that had fallen over me. This *end* seemed more like a beginning somehow.

Distracted by the man's last words, I slid, a pile of rocks reaching for me like teeth. My shoes, now buried under debris, hit something stiff. Pressing against it for leverage, I set to disentangling myself, when several feet in front of me I saw it, perched on its hind legs, gnawing into what appeared to be an ankle, protruding from the rock. Dazed, my gaze travelled from the rat to my impediment—a body hidden beneath the rubble. The rodent's pink tail curled around his grey middle, his cheeks full of the gory feast. Clearly, it wasn't scared of me, just taking it all in, evaluating, like I could be next on his menu. Then he went back to work, sinking his pointy teeth into the darkened flesh again.

My mouth twisted in disgust, revulsion worming its way up my throat. In my struggle to get free, I'd unearthed a rotten stench, and as I scrambled for purchase, I tried not to visualise what lay buried so close to me. My insides roiled. Two steps later, I fell to my knees, giving up the contents of my stomach. Wiping my mouth with my sleeve, I shuddered, tossing the rat another backward glance. It hadn't moved, just glared its beady little eyes at me and swallowed, as if wondering what all the fuss was about.

Above, a bird squawked. I startled, homing in as it circled in lazy sombre loops, before gliding down to pluck at its meal. After all, it wasn't in a hurry. There was no need. Not like the prey would scurry away somehow. They were stuck here, with their dead unseeing eyes, forever waiting, watching, in their open-air tombs. I turned my head, not wanting to see where the bird landed. Everything up here was fuel for nightmares. I already had more than enough. Eyes narrowed, focused straight ahead, I scuttled toward *home.*

* * *

While above, chaos stilled reigned, underground, a different sentiment presided. Jeremy, a man who'd worked closely with my father, set up headquarters on the outskirts of the Nest, mounting a resistance. Dad had sent the man actual paper records, documenting all his findings, and Jeremy had immediately dived in, committed to continuing the work my father started: ridding us of the corrupt Inner Circle, governing for the people and by the people, and not by the whims of malevolent beings from outer space bent on destruction of the human race, he reminded us. But our actual governing body still limped along in the brick-and-mortar buildings isolated on the streets above.

So, would both claim control at some point? Even I knew that would be a recipe for trouble in the not too distant days ahead, evidenced recently by the rush to sentence the condemned Inner Circle member.

I couldn't stop my dark chuckle, 'cause what should be clear-cut, raged and clashed inside me. Which side was I on? *Question everything…* My dad's words rang of truth like never before. In the depths of my mind, I acknowledged a third option, letting what had begun within me run its course, possibly leading to a different outcome instead.

I slid on a shirt and stepped into pants, determined to leave the life-defining decisions on simmer for now. They'd be there to pick up another day. Lately, Mom had encouraged me to sleep in, to gain back strength from what we'd been through: Dad's death. The Lost. My captivity, followed by the near end of us.

I gobbled down the cold breakfast Mom had probably left well over an hour ago, then plodded for the door.

"Wyatt." Her mom radar was working well today. I gritted my teeth as I whirled to face her. "What's up?"

"Nothing," I shrugged, impatient to be on my way. When I was busy, active, my thoughts tended not to stray. "But I am headed out for a while."

"To the Nest again?"

"That's right. Pete's letting me take over his booth for

the afternoon, and I'm determined to keep him in the black, while I'm there at the helm."

"I see." The layers of stress lining Mom's face had deepened since we'd survived the attack. Her hollowed eyes tracked mine, apprehension edging her voice. Confirmation of all my dad had predicted had decimated her world forever—the one she and Dad knew. Building it back? Who knew if we'd ever live in a world she'd recognise after what we'd all fought through.

And I wasn't so sure we should. After all, evolution is the natural order of things. And, if that were true, the entity would have its way, whether we got on board or waited on the sidelines. This one battle won or not. Maybe we were experiencing a brush with infinity; our trajectory here on Earth permanently changed.

Mom didn't want to hear that. She wanted to believe we could find our way back to the place we were before, given enough time. So, we don't talk about what's coming yet, only take each day one at a time, the two of us pretending, for now, that our lives are on the same path as they once were, even though we both know—along with the remnant of the Unfound that needed to emerge going forward—we'd never be there again.

"Dinner then, after?"

"Dinner," I agreed, and spun to leave.

My fingers curled into fists, punctuated at my side, eased open. The constant weight I carried on my shoulders lessened as I started out toward the energy that felt real…alive…when all else in my daily interactions reeked of impending doom. Dealing in black and white, entering into agreements, making exchanges, transactions adding to, or subtracting from, the bottom line, *that* was concrete. Something I could hang on to.

Not like the ramblings that came and went, taking me to the brink of insanity inside.

18

Wyatt

Another four weeks passed.

Life had a way of marching on. I still mourned my dad, the horrors Tess and I went through, and the brief relationship I had with Mason that altered me in ways I can't begin to understand, much less describe.

The doc had collected bits of the being's innards that had oozed onto surfaces, left behind as it had communed among us that fateful day. Each time I encountered the man, he had some new scrap of info or insight into what we may know about the extraterrestrial visitor someday. "I love my work," he exclaimed in passing in the corridor. I smiled, giving him a nod, and kept walking. Finding something that clicked like that was rare these days. The man's excitement was contagious, and I found myself jealous in a way. "Who knows what we'll discover from examining and analysing these samples," he yelled back at me, his voice fading, still on his tirade. His words hit home. More than we can possibly imagine. That's for sure.

The carnage and ruin above remained, with a few minor exceptions. The Lost had been gathered again, housed in some of the same facilities as before, but with assurances from the administrators their treatment would be humane this time. I shivered, as I always did, when contemplating my barely escaped fate: to roam around unconnected, oblivious for the rest of my days.

This was our generation's defining adversity. And dealing with the Lost of the population, one of our society's major challenges going forward. The blow dealt to us by a culmination of efforts—our government, under the control of an extraterrestrial being—was something we had to assume we'd face again.

Would we be ready? I wasn't confident of my place, unlike the others here in the Nest. Unlike my mom.

My mother thrived, basking in her element here as part of Dad's ongoing team. I'd never have guessed it, had I not seen the transformation with my own eyes. Of course, she'd always been a badass in her own way, managing staff, clients, and vendors to pull off perfection with her professionally managed events—every single time.

To make the switch to a no-nonsense, gun-toting, knife-wielding, boot-wearing vigilante… Well, sometimes it was hard to keep up, and it took some getting used to. Truthfully, Mom had always been up for any task. The rest of this was obviously her persona too. Me? Not so much.

Like a missing cog in a well-worn machine, she fit down here below. Dad had known it. Others could sense it, too. She had found her place among the growing team here, with a calm fortitude and an acceptance I didn't possess.

Dad had seen to our future involvement by mentioning it in our letters from him and through his appointee, Jeremy, who'd kept Mom and me in the loop at every turn.

Our underground team stayed connected to others in major cities by comms set up, using wired and radio telecommunications, still up and functional for the most part. This is where Jeremy wanted to plug me in initially, and I had a helluva lot to learn. These war rooms of sorts kept my attention when other interactions did not. Occupying my mind first and foremost with the concerns of the present, keeping my thoughts grounded to the here and now, was no small feat.

Another cause, independently tracking the massive numbers of the Lost, fed my need for involvement in something bigger than me. But it paled alongside the chasm that had ripped open in the universe, exposing mankind to more than a singular event. The being's immensity loomed, always there in the background, a constant reminder of its presence. Each day, I beat it into submission, remembering my dad and mother, who both worked to get me here, alive and in one piece.

Still, I can't help that it churns below the surface, and me—the son of the man who helped to author this alternative way forward—would feel this draw so intensely.

I reported to the war room, coming straight from my real-life training in the Nest. "You're doing great, kid," Jeremy commented, with a broad smile, as he slapped my shoulder and kept walking. I nodded a thanks in return, watching him take control, commanding the resources of the room. If there was hope, it resided within the connections here and within the possibility these relationships would build, growing to foster more.

It made sense that this was my father's ultimate dream—to triumph over that entity by the fruits borne of our humanity. From what I know now, though, I fear it will be no more than that…a dream. We're only a gnat in this thing's vision of the universe.

From across the room, Mom's gaze sought mine. Multiple emotions washed over her face—pride, love, and sadness all warring there. I let my mind sink back into the rhythm of the constant hum of the equipment, turning toward my task for now, becoming more comfortable in my niche with the predictability of the daily routine. As I tightened my focus to the immediate jobs needing completion today, at least during my waking hours, my thoughts felt settled, more my own, and I managed through the day.

The hours sped by, until nearing the end of my shift, I froze, red lights flashing, bleeding into the room, a loud blare almost hurling me from my skin. My heart pumping erratically, my jaw dropped open. I saw Jeremy running and screaming, pandemonium bursting to life throughout the place. Time slowed as I processed his next words. "Gas masks now! Everyone, our sensors have picked up poison spreading outside."

19

Wyatt

"We'll be safe here," Jeremy assured us, his words contradicting his tone. Even I knew we had no idea what these old tunnels would hold up against. My mind jump started, trying to connect the dots. While coworkers scurried about, the truth nagged my brain. They're finishing the job. It all fit. I fumbled, strapping the gas mask in place, watching the shell-shocked look of panic grip everyone's faces. Jeremy barked more orders, but my own agenda fought for my attention as I eased out a shaky breath, then another.

"Mom?" It took only a glimpse to feel the terror reflected in her eyes. I scrambled to my feet and hugged her tight. "I'm going to see what I can do," I screamed through the gas mask, the melee consuming us both.

"Don't you dare go out there," she shouted through a sob. "You can't fight this, and I won't lose you too."

Around the masks encumbering us, I squeezed her once more. "Stay here," I encouraged, trying to steady my voice. "They need your wisdom, your guidance. I'll be right back."

Her mouth formed an *O*, widened in another scream, but I slipped from her hands easily. As confusion and turmoil caught up with us, I used it to disappear, to lose myself in the mounting crowds. Looking around, pushing my way through the clutter of people, I saw virtually all wore gas masks. Of course, it made sense. Thinking back, they'd been prepared long before us, the brainwashed public.

The people—the Lost, the sick, the grieving, and everybody in between. What would become of them now? Out here in the Nest, closer to the streets, I could hear little snippets of sound from aboveground, so I shoved harder, my body and boots clearing a path.

Propelled forward by the motion of the masses and my own need to be free, soon I wasn't sure how much time had passed. I reached the old familiar subway cars, the iron rungs in sight that led to the door, the passageway to this latest standoff with extinction. My steps echoed in the space as I tromped the last stretch and, stilling my advance, I homed in on the broken voices, dreading what I'd face.

My foot hit the ladder; my hands clung to the rungs, and going through the motions, I started to ascend; one second climbing, then petrified, I stopped. Beyond our enclosure, the horrified cries and muffled screams intensified, gunfire piercing the howling and wailing in their wake. God, what could I do about this…annihilation? *Nothing…* The voice shouted inside my head.

Poised there, I wavered, trapped by the guttural cries, the pounding at the door, the pleads for mercy, when my thoughts were interrupted by rough hands yanking me backwards. Bound among a trio of men, they lowered me down to Jeremy and mom. My gaze locked with hers. She looked like she'd never forgive me. I averted my eyes.

"You can't save them. *We* can't save them," Jeremy spoke in the midst of the carnage, his anger barely controlled as he shot me a glare.

"But them is us," I spat, biting back tears. Staggering as I tried to walk, I hunched my shoulders against the ongoing cacophony, while just beyond our reach, rampant death claimed the streets.

"Is it better that we all die, leaving no one at all?" Jeremy yelled, grabbing me by the neck. "Because if you open that door, me, you, your mom, hell, all of us…we're gone too." He growled out a breath and released me. "This was a coordinated attack. Other major cities have reported in. We've got to survive." He gave my shoulders a hard squeeze. "Persevere for humanity's sake. The small bands of us across the PS are all that's left."

My body on auto pilot, I shrugged. As the cold, slivery pockets of death multiplied inside me, it already felt like it was over.

Later, alone in my room, I slid down against the wall, arms hugging my knees; no way would I let sleep come for me now. Visions of poisonous gas, with its stench-ridden promise of the end, ate away at the flesh from emaciated bodies, the live action battle still ongoing, never-ending in my head. Whenever I drifted off for a minute, the death cries joined in, the gory scenes painting the insides of my eyelids. It was hopeless. I'd never be right again.

My mom had come and gone several times, trying to get me to eat—an activity my stomach vehemently rejected so, finally, at my urging, she'd given me some space.

Silence descended.

In the solitude, I floundered, searching for something to hang onto besides misery…besides death. More was out there, beyond; I was never more certain of anything. We'd taken only the first step. Much more existed, real and tangible, just outside the veil.

A void yawned within me, a product of the death, destruction, and the strange link I'd encountered intersecting the two. Waiting and watching, awkwardly searching with this fledgling bond locked inside me somehow, I let it take me, coming alive with a connection I couldn't deny. *Just for a while*, I reasoned. To chase away the desolation and despair that preyed upon me now.

This time the connection yanked me forward, tearing, slashing into the innards of my brain. My body jolted, writhing with pain. A tiny moment of panic set in. What had I done? Could I break free? If not, what did it matter? Little else remained for me here. My tension eased.

My gaze adjusted to the sight. Before me was its centre, a pulsing, beating core, and even though my humanity called me, I couldn't turn away, the need to know more driving me onwards. Sliding through sinewy cords, traversing splatters of flesh, the fluid motion carried me in deeper as I peered through the murkiness. My heart hammered a reply, my senses on high alert, because swarming ahead, extending out from the nothingness, were its appendages, flailing, thrashing in their approach.

From inside the morass, slithery bands plunged into my brain, the joining visceral, innate, right in a way. Reminding myself to breathe, I gulped down air, fighting intuitively against the breech. But my struggle was short-lived. Useless. The entity had me…

I was his.

What this meant—how I would evolve from our interaction—I couldn't guess just yet. My only clarity, staring at the vastness around me—I hungered, even yearned for what it gave. I settled into the network, ingesting, sucking in what it granted. As knowledge washed through me and I wrestled with each new wave, I wondered how much longer the human parts of me could endure. Already the shadowy lines of its cold alien form had coalesced with mine.

I was being remade.

20

Words stuck in my throat. "Wyatt… Wyatt! Wake up. Oh my God, someone help him!"

The sight of him—it was hard to take in. Two weeks had passed since the second worst day of my life, and still not much change in my son. I couldn't help pressuring Doc, who was almost as manic as I was.

"Tell me. Anything. I need something of substance to cling to."

He shook his head, pressing his lips into a straight line.

"Okay, not a good sign."

"Truth is Ellie, me and the experts who I've consulted haven't made a great deal of headway. Remember, resources are stretched tight, but we did discover an anomaly on one of his brain scans yesterday—"

"And you didn't tell me?"

"Now hold on Ellie. I wanted to find out as much as possible first." Charlie clicked a series of keys on his computer. "Come, take a look."

The detailed picture of my son's brain was just a haze of muted colours to me. "What am I looking at here?" I asked, a mixture of fear and hope creeping into my voice.

"Makes more of an impression when you compare the two." Doc arranged the scan taken two weeks ago next to the one taken yesterday. "Now, what do you see?"

I gasped, drawing in closer to the images. "What's happening there?" I asked, pointing to the enlarging mass, scrutinising the two.

Doc's mouth bent into a frown. "The million-dollar question. I can tell you what it's not. Not cancer or a degenerative disease. Also ruled out a foreign object. The rest is just a guess…"

His eyebrows jacked up as I met his gaze. "Okay. Give me what you got."

"Well," he exhaled a long breath and pointed at the latest x-ray, "without getting too technical, the field of expansion here corresponds to the place where cognitive intelligence resides inside the brain. Appears your son's ability in that area has skyrocketed."

"That doesn't sound so awful. But why then won't he wake up?"

"I don't have a clue, Ellie. Other than it doesn't appear that the process is finished with him yet. More detailed areas of development emerge with each additional scan. It's incredible really."

I clutched my son's hand. "Come back to me, Wyatt. Don't you dare ditch me."

My shoulders slumped as Doc continued. "Don't give up. My team and I won't either. Wyatt is made of tough stuff. There's always hope."

Son-of-a-bitch, Wyatt… What's up with you? I pushed past the door and into the hallway, reaching for my recently negotiated contraband. With the cigarette between my lips, I cupped my hands around the light and took a deep draw. God, how long has it been? The scent and taste of tobacco meandered its way through me, lingering as I inhaled. Remembering my old nemesis, I held my breath, then exhaled. Damn, I've missed you. Just what I needed. My fingers shook as I contemplated my son's prognosis. What the hell was I gonna do? I huffed out a sigh and then took another drag.

If not for Wyatt, all this would be pointless. We're not guaranteed tomorrow or even the next ten minutes. I know that. But you, son, *need* to make it. God… I slammed my eyes shut. "Scott, help, please… Let our son live."

21

Wyatt

My chest tightened, my eyes falling shut. *I'm here,* I spilled forth, in a clumsy attempt at speech with the manifestation inside the growing abyss. Blurred from my current surroundings, surrendered to the darkness coiled between us, I opened myself, not fully cognisant of what lay ahead. From the perspective of new birth, the possibilities endless as I hovered there, wavering between waking and dreaming…wandering between the Lost and Found.

J. W. Garrett

J W GARRETT is a multi-award-winning author. Initiated into fantasy after reading *The Hobbit* in elementary school, she has been hooked ever since. She writes speculative fiction from the sunny beaches of Jacksonville, Florida, but loves the mountains of Virginia where she was born. Her writings include novels, short stories, and poetry. Since completing *Remeon's Crusade*, the third book in her sci-fi fantasy series, Realms of Chaos, she has been hard at work on the next instalment. When she's not hanging out with her characters, her favourite activities are reading, running and spending time with family.

Bibliography

Caramelized Pecan Cookie Holiday Hideaway, The Wild Rose Press, 2021

Hidden In the Arms of Time, 2018

Jibbernocky, Black Hare Press, 2020

Remeon's Crusade, BHC Press, 2020

Remeon's Destiny, BHC Press, 2018

Remeon's Quest, BHC Press, 2019

The Fae of Boots and Laces, 2018

Contact

Website: www.jwgarrett.com
Facebook: @jwgarrettwriter
Instagram: @jlwgarrett
Twitter: @garrettjlw

Black Hare Press

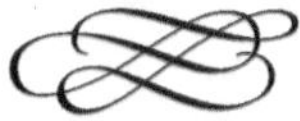

BLACK HARE PRESS is a small, independent publisher based in Melbourne, Australia.

Founded in 2018, our aim has always been to champion emerging authors from all around the globe and offer opportunities for them to participate in speculative fiction and horror short story anthologies.

Connect: linktr.ee/blackharepress